SPRING
Love

A Wildfire Book

WILDFIRE TITLES FROM SCHOLASTIC

Love Comes to Anne by Lucille S. Warner
I'm Christy by Maud Johnson
Beautiful Girl by Elisabeth Ogilvie
Superflirt by Helen Cavanagh
Dreams Can Come True by Jane Claypool Miner
I've Got a Crush on You by Carol Stanley
An April Love Story by Caroline B. Cooney
Dance with Me by Winifred Madison
Yours Truly, Love, Janie by Ann Reit
The Summer of the Sky-Blue Bikini by Jill Ross Klevin
The Best of Friends by Jill Ross Klevin
The Voices of Julie by Joan Oppenheimer
Second Best by Helen Cavanagh
A Place for Me by Helen Cavanagh
Sixteen Can Be Sweet by Maud Johnson
Take Care of My Girl by Carol Stanley
Lisa by Arlene Hale
Secret Love by Barbara Steiner
Nancy & Nick by Caroline B. Cooney
Wildfire Double Romance by Diane McClure Jones
Senior Class by Jane Claypool Miner
Cindy by Deborah Kent
Too Young to Know by Elisabeth Ogilvie
Junior Prom by Patricia Aks
Saturday Night Date by Maud Johnson
He Loves Me Not by Caroline Cooney
Good-bye, Pretty One by Lucille S. Warner
Just a Summer Girl by Helen Cavanagh
The Impossible Love by Arlene Hale
Sing About Us by Winifred Madison
The Searching Heart by Barbara Steiner
Write Every Day by Janet Quin-Harkin
Christy's Choice by Maud Johnson
The Wrong Boy by Carol Stanley
Make a Wish by Nancy Smiler Levinson
The Boy for Me by Jane Claypool Miner
Class Ring by Josephine Wunsch
Phone Calls by Ann Reit
Just You and Me by Ann Martin
Homecoming Queen by Winifred Madison
Holly in Love by Carolina B. Cooney
Spring Love by Jennifer Sarasin

SPRING
Love

JENNIFER SARASIN

SCHOLASTIC INC.
New York Toronto London Auckland Sydney

Cover Photograph by **Owen Brown**

ISBN 0-590-40345-1

12 11 10 9 8 7 6 5 4 3 2 1   6 7 8 9/8 0 1/9

Printed in the U.S.A.   06

For my father — then and now . . .

SPRING
Love

O^{ne}

The apartment was so terribly silent, Becca could hear the creak of her new shoes on the floorboards. The shoes her mother bought for her just before she left for Michigan. "You have to look great for senior year, sweetie," Rachel Walters had insisted as they stood on Fifth Avenue, wondering which store to cover next. "And you want to look nice for your father, too." And this very morning, her mother had flown away, out of Becca's life, for good. Her parents were divorcing, and Becca was stuck with her father.

Of course, they told her, it didn't have to be that way. There was a terrific high school right near the University of Michigan campus, where her mother was going to get her master's degree. Becca could transfer there for senior year and spend the summer before college with her father. But what kind of choice was that? Leaving all her friends, her great school, the apartment where she'd spent her entire sixteen years? After Manhattan, Ann Arbor, Michigan, would feel like Siberia.

Becca stared at the print on the living room wall. She remembered clearly when they had bought it, after a summer weekend on Cape Cod. The three of them together, laughing, eating steamed clams, swimming in the ocean — icy even on a hot August day. *Weren't they happy then?* she asked herself, touching the frame with one finger. *Didn't they love each other then?*

Well, to be honest, Becca had to admit that her parents' marriage had never been anything to write romances about. Her father, Dr. David Walters, was a small, quiet, conservative man, very stern and overprotective. Sometimes, Becca didn't think she knew who he was. He'd always been like a stranger in the house.

But her mother, lovely Rach, was different. She was Becca's best friend, and always had been. She was pretty and smart and funny, the kind of pal you could really talk to. One of Becca's favorite pastimes was sitting on her parents' bed, watching her mother dress for the day. Rachel had an eye for unusual, dramatic clothes, and they draped around her long, leggy frame as though they'd been custom-made for her. Becca, on the other hand, was short like her father and shaped something like a pear. Even when she lost weight, it came off in all the wrong places.

Becca sighed and wandered from the living room to the dining room. With her father making rounds at the hospital as he did every Saturday morning, the apartment was all hers. All seven cold, lonely rooms of it. She ran her hand along the side of the shiny oak dining room table. "Why are you waxing it," she'd asked her mother just two nights ago, "if you're going away?"

"So your father won't get mad," was Rachel's curt response.

Why did he get mad so much? Becca had learned over the years that the best course of action was to stay out of his way. It wasn't like he was nasty or bad or anything, he was just super-critical. Whether it was her violin practice or her grades or her clothes or the way she'd casually answer a question about a friend — he'd have some correction to make. The big Schoolmaster in the Sky. Every once in a long while, though, he'd tell a joke or act kind of silly or drop a hasty kiss on Becca's head. Sometimes, she recalled, he was even tender.

When she was little, he'd taught her to ride a bike, and he'd been so patient, waiting until she said it was all right to take the training wheels off. Whenever she was sick, there was Daddy, ready with an aspirin or a thermometer or a little bedside manner. He really was a good doctor, Becca thought. He liked taking care of things, making things better. And when he was concerned and thoughtful like that, Becca really admired him.

So why did he have to be so awful the rest of the time? *Wow, a whole year alone with him!* It suddenly occurred to her that they'd have to eat all their meals together and spend all their evenings together, unless Becca had a date or something. (Maybe her father would never let her go out on a date!) He probably didn't even know that high school seniors were supposed to have a social life. She could just imagine bringing a guy in to meet her father before they left for the evening. He'd sit in his armchair in the living room, the one that nobody else ever sat in, and smooth his neat, clipped mustache. Then he'd scowl under his bushy eyebrows and scrutinize the young man as though he were one of his patients on the examining table. "Pizza?" he'd ask as though it were some kind of Martian food. "You're taking her out for pizza? Do you think that's advisable?"

Oh, come on! Becca suddenly laughed aloud. *Now you're being unreasonable. He's not an ogre or anything.*

At least, not all the time.

She wandered around the dining room and down the corridor to her parents' room. She paused when she got to the door. This was the room where they'd slept together, made love — well, at least once — and finally grown apart. They weren't anything alike and had so little in common that Becca wondered why they'd ever gotten married and stayed together for seventeen years. Gingerly, she took one step across the threshold, hugging herself tightly against the flood of emotion threatening to burst out of her.

"This is horrible!" she said aloud. "This shouldn't be happening! How could they do this to me now! All they had to do was wait one more stupid year and I would have graduated and gotten out of their way. I mean, they waited this long, so why couldn't they wait a little longer?" She walked to the mirror and spoke to her image. "It's really dumb."

The bathroom was behind the bed. She closed her eyes and sniffed. There it was, the scent of her mother's perfume still hanging in the air. It was everywhere — in the closets, the hampers, the medicine chest where she kept the bottle of Chamade. Becca pressed her forehead against the glass of the cabinet, and as she opened her eyes, she noticed a few strands of her mother's hair lying on the sink. She was mesmerized by the sight. Rachel had wonderful, silky red hair with just the right amount of curl in it, so that all she had to do after she washed it was comb it into place. Becca's hair was thin and flyaway, just like her father's, and it was plain, drab brown. Her romantic mother used to call it "pastel mink," but Becca knew better — it was mousy.

She ripped a Kleenex from the box on a shelf and wiped up the hair, then crumpled the tissue and threw it in the toilet. In the one short week since Becca had decided not to go to Michigan with her mother, everything was different. It was horrible, but it was true. There would be no more girl talk or sharing of clothes, as they sometimes had, or talking late into the night about Becca's problems or about boys. That was all over. Now Becca was the woman of the house, and she'd better grow up fast and do things right or her father would have an awful lot more to criticize. Of course, he'd taken care of the details already. He'd hired a housekeeper so quickly, Becca wondered whether things had been in the works for months and her parents had just been waiting to tell her. This stranger would come in on Tuesdays and Thursdays and clean the apartment and cook enough stuff to put in the freezer so they'd have dinners for the next few days.

Don't cry, Becca told herself firmly, walking out of the bathroom. She wouldn't allow herself to look in her mother's closet to see all the empty hangers. She wouldn't peer into the empty drawers to smell the sachet scent that was purely and simply her mother.

Her mother had gone. Flew the coop, abandoned ship, run away from home.

"That was a disgusting thing to do!" Becca slammed the door of her parents' room behind her, fuming, filled with a rage so enormous she thought it would spill all over the room. What was she feeling so sorry and moony for, anyway? She was good and angry — neglected and left alone and furious! She deserved better than this! It wasn't her problem, after all, that her parents were two nice people who couldn't get along anymore.

She walked slowly back into the living room and sank down onto the midnight blue velvet couch. Her brows knit and a lump of hard misery rose in her throat. Life wasn't supposed to be this way. Parents were supposed to take care of kids and love them and show them the right way to grow up. As far as Becca was concerned, Rachel and David Walters had never learned how to be adults. Neither one could compromise or see the other's point of view. So Becca — serious, clever, amusing Becca — got to be the arbitrator, the one in the middle of every fight. Well, at least that wouldn't happen anymore. Now she'd be on the receiving end of all her father's wrath.

Oh, why hadn't she gone with her mother? Things were always carefree and fun with Rachel, because she had a gift for seeing the most ordinary items as magical and special. A plain old sofa cushion became a medieval shield; a stale bagel turned into a ring toss — that is, when Dr. Walters wasn't around to spoil the game.

Well, she'd see her mother at Christmas, and she'd talk to her on the phone at least twice a week. Then they'd have the whole summer together before Becca started college — that's what they'd decided. It was probably better not to be shifted from one parent to the other every month, like some divorced kids Becca knew. Senior year was so important, and the continuity of friends and places to go and things to do was really vital.

"I guess I can hold out till Christmas," she said aloud. Not that it was going to be easy, but what else could she do? There would be schoolwork to keep her busy, and her violin, and her part-time job in the language lab. Too bad the lab closed at four every afternoon. If Becca had her way, she'd stay out until dinner-time and lock herself in her room to study as soon as the meal was over. Anything to stay away from her father.

The phone rang and Becca jumped. Her heart was racing as she dashed into the hall-way to answer it. There was nothing as spooky as a phone ringing away in an empty apart-ment.

"Yes? Hello."

"Hello. Is this the Walters residence?" It was an older woman's voice.

"That's right. Who is this, please?"

"Am I addressing the woman of the house?"

"Well, I . . . oh, no, I'm just the . . ." Becca cleared her throat, feeling awkward and out of place. She immediately had a picture of a tiny little girl wearing her mother's hat and shoes, with bright red lipstick smeared all over her face. "Yes, that's me," she admitted sul-lenly.

"Good. Now, Mrs. Walters, I know that you and your husband are readers of *The New York Times*, and I wanted to tell you about this one-time offer for a special subscription rate, if you act right now."

"I'm *not* Mrs. Walters!" Becca snapped, slamming the phone down. She held the receiver on its cradle so it wouldn't jump up and hit her in the face. She was crying, and she'd promised herself not to. When her parents first told her, she'd cried on and off for days. She began to see how terribly this upset them, so she stopped — to please them. Crying wasn't like her; she'd always gotten through bad times with her quirky sense of humor. That was her buffer against the world, and it was a great disguise when she didn't want to share her feelings. She'd just pretend she was somebody else, without Becca Walters's problems, that's all.

Now a dumb phone call had wrecked all her good intentions.

"Stop it, you hear me," she said severely. Then, for effect, she added, "You have real depressive tendencies, you know that?"

"Vell, doctor, und vat do you prescribe?" she replied.

"Two miocardamom tablets, 500 cc daily, taken at bedtime and on awakening in the morning, washed down with a glass of silly-ciberon."

"Sounds good," she murmured, wiping away the final tears. "But maybe a candy bar would do the trick just as well."

Sure. No sense hanging around an empty

apartment. It was a nice day — she remembered seeing the sun when she got up that morning. She only had two more days of freedom before school started, so she really should be out tooling around Manhattan as much as she could.

She decided on jeans and a candy-striped short-sleeved blouse, with flat white sandals so she could walk for miles if she chose to. Maybe she'd call Judy to have lunch someplace near Bloomingdale's. Then an afternoon of window-shopping and reading reviews outside movie theaters. Then home at last, for her first solitary meal with her father. What fun!

Locking the door behind her, Becca took the elevator to the lobby and walked out into the sunny morning. Her mother was airborne right now, flying away like a bird going south for the winter. Except where she was going, it was going to be frigid. *I hope she has enough sweaters*, Becca mused as she turned toward Lexington Avenue. Then she smiled to herself. *Hey, your mom's a big girl now — she can take care of herself.*

But can she? Becca wondered. For all her mother's wild spirit and independence, she was pretty helpless at times. Never good with money, she'd accepted an allowance from her husband up until the day she finished Betty Friedan's *The Feminine Mystique*. Then, all at once, she got liberated. But she still was lousy at managing money and invariably had to ask Becca to balance her checkbook every month.

At the corner of Eighty-fourth Street, Becca entered the Good News Stationery Store and browsed along the paperback racks before posting herself in front of the candy shelves. *This is terrible. I'm going to break out if I eat chocolate*, she warned herself.

But I deserve it. I feel so rotten.

Becca was not at all surprised when she arrived at a compromise several moments later and selected a package of mixed nuts and raisins. She was so sensible, so much in control of every situation! *Wow, are you dull!* she said inwardly as she smiled and paid Mr. Danzig.

"How are you, Rebecca?" he asked, puffing on his stub of a smelly cigar.

"Just fine, thanks, Mr. Danzig," she lied.

"So how's your mama, I never see her anymore?"

Becca frowned and said nothing. There was nothing to say, really.

Two

"I think this is just the stupidest arrangement." Becca's friend Judy was marching stolidly down the first-floor corridor of Halsted High, waving her program card in the air. "I mean, giving us gym fifth period on the sixth floor, so we have to race around to get to French on the second floor all grimy and disgusting. It's insane!"

Becca was walking beside her friend, lost in a haze. The only thought on her mind this second day of the new term was how to avoid going home. *I could take the subway and it might get stuck for hours,* she thought. The worst part about that fantasy was that her father would still ask why she hadn't called.

"Fifty feet below the ground, Daddy? Where was I supposed to find a phone?"

"You didn't even try."

"Becca, dearheart, are you awake? Hey, I'm talking to you!" Judy was grinning again. It was never like her to pout for long. Judy and Becca had known each other since they were in third grade, although Becca wouldn't have called them really good friends. Judy was like a butterfly, always zooming from one subject to another, always fussing over her looks or her plans. Of course, as Becca had often confided to her mother, it was easy to be vain with looks like Judy's. She was petite but wore clothes like a model. Next to her red sweater set and pleated plaid kilt, Becca's black turtleneck and gray wraparound skirt looked positively like discards from the Salvation Army. And Judy's skin! It was clear and smooth as a baby's, accenting her deep-set ice-blue eyes and high cheekbones. But her most striking feature was her hair. It was a honey-blond fall of pure radiance, and it was so long she could sit on it. Judy *was* slightly overweight, but as she repeatedly told Becca, it was only baby fat and would fall off of its own accord on graduation day. Becca got a kick out of

Judy's attitude toward life, mostly because it was about a hundred and eighty degrees away from Becca's. Judy saw the glass as half-full; Becca saw it as more than half-empty.

"Listen, this is no time to fade out on me," Judy insisted as they made their way down the stairs to the locker room. They were both advanced music students, and one study hall a week was given over to Becca's violin and Judy's guitar practice. "I cannot tell you all the wonders in store," Judy gushed, fiddling with the combination of her lock, missing it, cursing, and starting again. "Senior year is like opening a chest of buried treasure."

"I know," Becca smiled, extracting her violin case from her locker. Maybe her violin could fall on Lexington Avenue and a truck would hit it and she'd have to go with the driver to his company's office in Queens to fill out all the insurance forms.

"I'll get in the mood, I promise, dearheart," she said, calling her friend by the rather theatrical term they had picked up from a Neil Simon movie last spring. "Now, let's get going, okay? If I'm going to play that Bach suite in assembly, I better get cracking."

"Wait, hey, wait a sec. Stay right here." Judy slammed her locker shut and pulled her into the main basement area, where all the candy machines were located. She jerked her friend

over to the niche that contained the water fountain and shook her cloak of hair over one
shoulder while she bent to take a long drink.
Then she looked up anxiously and glanced
down the hall.

"What is it?" Becca hugged her violin and
walked around to peer in the same direction.
Judy yanked her back into the niche with a
sharp intake of breath.

"I knew he was coming about now. Just
hold on — we've got time," Judy said, pressing one hand firmly on Becca's back until she
had no choice but to bend down and take a
drink.

Just then, the door at the bottom of the
stairwell opened and three guys walked out,
followed seconds later by a fourth. They were
laughing together and didn't see the girls until
Judy popped out of their niche like a jack-in-
the-box, almost tripping the first boy, Kevin
McGiness.

"Oh, sorry," she said, too loudly. He blushed
to the roots of his carrot-red hair. Becca looked
the other way, trying to disassociate herself
from this madwoman. *Judy was always silly,
but she was never boy-crazy*, she thought
angrily.

"That's okay," the second boy grinned.

"Hey, I like surprises like that," the third
one added. He was Steve Simon, a real loudmouth. Becca knew him from history class.

The fourth boy paid no attention to this interchange and kept on walking. His friends followed him with a variety of muttered comments. Becca could just guess what they were saying.

"Dreamy, right?" Judy sighed as they disappeared.

"Which one?"

"Mark, of course. Mark Shuman — the fourth one in line. What's wrong with your eyes?"

"The little one with the red cheeks?"

"Becca! Mark's at least five-eight. He may not be a giant, but he's got everything in all the right places. He's all there."

Becca couldn't help herself. She burst out laughing — the first time she'd laughed in a week. "You sound just like a guy describing a girl! You do have the oddest way of putting things, dearheart." She shook her head and started walking toward the staircase.

"But he *is* gorgeous!" Judy insisted, hurrying after her. "Those crinkly eyes, those arched nostrils. But what really gets me is his European cheeks."

"Huh?" Becca frowned, taking the stairs to the second-floor practice rooms two at a time.

"You know, the way he always looks like he's just come in out of the cold. All rosy and cute."

Becca couldn't believe this was really her

old friend Judy talking. She'd turned into a goon over the summer! "I really never noticed," she said, stopping to glance at her watch. "Come on, we're really late. I have to get to language lab early after practice to talk to Kizner, and you know how punctual he is."

"You are something." Judy flipped her hair over one shoulder to reveal a tiny gold stud earring. "You're like a zombie — not listening, not noticing. And you look dreadful, if you don't mind my saying so. Like you haven't slept in a week. What's the matter, Becca? Don't you like me anymore?"

Becca bit her lip. Should she tell her? Judy could be sympathetic even if she was awfully self-centered. She'd usually been a good listener. Of course, that was junior year and that was the old Judy. "Well, see, there's a little trouble at home," she muttered at last.

"What kind of trouble?"

Becca had to say it. She'd come this far and she honestly did want to tell somebody. "My mom left my dad," she blurted out.

"What!" Judy practically screamed. "You mean like in *Kramer vs. Kramer*?"

"Shush!" Becca looked down the stairwell self-consciously, but everyone had already gone to class or study hall, and they were alone. "It's not at all like that. They were, uh, getting ready for a divorce for a long time.

They really should have done it a long time ago," she added bravely, hoping she sounded extremely practical about the whole thing. "But you know, they stayed together for the sake of the child."

"Wow," Judy breathed. "Your mom split! Did she run off with a tennis pro or something?"

"She went to Michigan to get her master's degree," Becca said angrily. "Look, this is not some grade B movie. This is my life!"

"Yeah, hey, I know that." Judy was suddenly sobered. She reached out and put a hand on Becca's shoulder. "This must be real tough on you, right? I didn't even know you were that tight with your father that you'd want to stay with him instead of your mom."

"Well, I . . ." Here Becca had to choose her words carefully. "It's going to be great getting to know each other better." She nodded. "We were . . . we actually haven't been all that close, but it's working out fantastically."

Liar.

"Gee, well, I know my mom will want you to come for dinner as much as he'll let you. And my sister can be a terrific help, I know it," Judy rushed on nervously. Becca had the impression that she really wasn't all that keen on knowing every gruesome detail. It was pretty embarrassing, any way you looked at it.

"Oh, why your sister?" They climbed to the top of the stairs and pushed open the door to the second floor. They walked quickly to the practice rooms, searching around for two empty ones.

"She's a psych major at NYU, didn't I tell you? She has some great insight into other people's problems. There's this one course on human interaction, and I'm sure she'd let you borrow the books. Like *Open Marriage* and *Creative Divorce* and *Living and Loving After Divorce*. You really ought to digest that sort of information soon, Becca." Judy sounded terribly concerned, and Becca couldn't help but give her friend a wry smile.

"I should, huh? May I ask why?" She had her hand on the doorknob of the practice room, but she had to hear her friend's response.

"You don't want to repeat your parents' mistakes, do you?" Judy demanded in a shocked voice. "Do you know what the statistics are about kids of divorced parents getting divorced themselves?"

"High, I'm sure."

"Stratospheric!" Judy exclaimed, throwing her arms out to encompass whole nations of divorced people. "It's incredible — you wouldn't believe."

"Well then, I guess I just have to be the one to break the mold," Becca scoffed. "Listen, I gotta go. Thanks for the ear."

"Anytime, honest. Hey, Becca," she added before turning away. "You know what you need? Something wonderful to take your mind off all this. Like a boyfriend."

Becca cleared her throat and stared at the floor. "That looks very nice on paper, dearheart, but statistics are against that happening during the first week of school."

"You can never tell," Judy sang out, waltzing down the corridor to the next available room. "You just keep your eyes open, sweetie."

Becca closed the door behind her and placed her books and violin case on the nearest desk. How absurd — to imagine any stupid how-to books could help! And a boyfriend. As if Becca could just walk up to somebody with "European cheeks" — what was his name, Mark? — and say gee-I-know-it-would-be-wonderful - therapy-for-me-to-spend-lots-of-time-with-you-and-how-about-a-date? How ridiculous!

Judy definitely didn't understand. This was just something she was going to have to live with, Becca decided as she flipped the case open and withdrew her instrument and bow. First she wiped the violin carefully, then she took out her rosin cube and began to rub the bow. When she was ready, she picked up the violin and began tuning. These actions were automatic, easy to accomplish without any thought whatsoever. But when she got her music out and opened to the first page of the Bach suite, her eyes filled and she couldn't see the notes.

"Oh, what's the use! I'll never learn this," she grumbled, making a halfhearted attempt to play while talking aloud. Good thing there was no one around to hear her. "This is the first sign of madness, dearheart," she whispered softly. Then she gritted her teeth and dug into the Bach for all she was worth. It sounded terrible, but at least she got through it. Her teacher was always insisting she get from beginning to end. *Just like life*, she thought philosophically.

She concentrated on making a beautiful sound, but she didn't feel at all beautiful inside, and it showed in her playing. The greatest musicians, her teacher told her time and again, are in love with themselves, and they pour their own beauty right out of this box through the bow. At that moment, there was a loud pop. Her D string had burst.

She was startled when the bell rang for the end of the period, but in a way she was relieved. This simply wasn't her day for practicing, and besides, she had to talk to Mr. Kizner before language lab got under way. She'd been working for him for two and a half years, and she loved the job almost as much as she did him. Even though he taught the deadest subject of all — Latin — he was generally regarded by the students as their best friend. He had a fantastic sense of humor and he really cared about kids.

Packing up her case and grabbing her things, Becca rushed into the hall, joining the flood of students milling around, chatting, laughing, promising to meet somewhere for a Coke. Becca was invisible, though, she knew it. No one saw her or said hello. *Does it show?* she wondered unhappily. *Am I just so different now that I have nothing in common with these people anymore?* Judy had said she looked awful, and she was right, of course.

Mournfully, she climbed the stairs behind a group of laughing girls who were discussing Mr. Granville, the attractive new math teacher. When she got to the fourth floor, she took a right turn and entered the language lab, her heart pounding. What would Mr. Kizner say when she told him she was quitting? And what was she going to do after she left the lab? If only it stayed open all night for the real grinds determined to pick up Russian or Spanish in a week or so. Then she could live in the lab, doling out cassettes, fixing machines, cataloging new tapes. But the lab closed promptly at four — practically the middle of the day. Last year that had been just fine, but now . . . She couldn't go home to an empty house and wait for her father. What was she supposed to do? Greet him at the door with his pipe and slippers? Except that he didn't smoke a pipe. No, there was nothing to do but quit the lab and find something that would take up a lot more of her time.

She was standing, hugging her books, her violin tucked firmly under her arm, when a voice behind her boomed, "Lab's open for the day. Get your tapes here! Hurry, hurry, ladies and gents. Be the first on your block to learn the new international language, Upper Mongolian Swahili Suisse."

Mr. Morton Kizner barreled into the room, his coattails covered with chalk from leaning against the blackboard, as he always did. There was something to be said for his sloppy dress code, Becca thought, since it put the kids more at ease. Morton Kizner was a small, wiry little man, and his arms were always jutting out at odd angles. He walked briskly to his desk and Becca followed him.

"Uh, excuse me," she began timidly. A couple of kids were already lined up at the lending desk, and it was her job to check out whatever tapes they wanted. But she simply had to get this over with first.

"Three P.M., Ms. Walters," he reminded her.

"Oh, yeah, I mean, I know, Mr. Kizner. But

I just wondered if I could ask you something."
She glanced nervously at the growing line of
impatient students.

"Shoot."

"Well, it's actually that I have to tell you
something. I'm . . . I have to give up this job,
I'm afraid. Of course, I'll finish out the week
or stay until you get a replacement."

"Don't tell me you've just been assigned to
the astronaut program and need your after-
noons off?" he asked, very seriously.

"Oh, well, no." She couldn't even smile,
even though she knew he was being funny.
"You see, I need a paying job this year."

"Yes?" He encouraged her to go on with a
questioning look.

"Things have sort of changed at home and,
um, the money would come in handy."

Did he know her father was a fancy Park
Avenue doctor? He must think she was a real
flake. This was awful. Just because her parents
were getting divorced was no reason to turn
into a pathological liar.

"What kind of position are you considering,
Ms. Walters? Maybe I can top their offer."

"I don't . . . well, I can't really say I have
any possibilities yet. But it has to pay some
money and last till about six P.M. every night,"
she confided.

"Oh, I see," Mr. Kizner said with a raised

eyebrow, glancing over at the disgruntled kids waiting in line. "You'll do anything as long as it keeps you off the streets, right?"

"Right," she nodded.

"You know, I might have an idea for you. It's no guarantee, but the work is very similar to what you've been doing here. Mark Shuman just mentioned to me after class today that they need a new trainee over where he works."

A strange feeling went through her when she heard Mark's name again. Why was she so affected by a name, for heaven's sake? Must be brain rot.

"Oh? Where's that?" Mark — he was the one Judy was so nuts about. Wouldn't she be surprised if Becca got a job at the same place he worked!

"It's at the New York Recording for the Blind. They put books on tape, you know. I have no idea what the salary is, but if they need someone in a hurry, you probably have a good chance of getting the job. I'll ask Mark for you. Now if you don't move it and take care of those ravenous animals over there"— he nodded toward the kids on line — "you will get no reference from me, young lady."

"Yes, oh, sure. And thanks, Mr. Kizner. You don't know what this means to me!"

"Believe me," he said, beating his breast like a bereaved father, "I won't be gaining a son,

I'll be losing a daughter. Get to work, Becca!"
he shouted.

She plowed into the rest of the afternoon,
feeling for the first time in days that there was
some shred of sunlight left in the sky, some
reason for hope. Yet, when she closed down
the lab at four and started for the door, un-
happiness fell back on her like a shroud.

*Maybe I could be right outside the Russian
embassy when some anti-Communists come
by and barricade the place and everyone who
was outside when it happened would get taken
hostage.*

But as there seemed to be little chance of a
subway breakdown or a terrorist takeover,
Becca decided to kill time by walking the
fifteen blocks home from school. She dawdled
and stared into store windows, not really seeing their displays. She walked along as though
there were weights attached to her shoes, and
still it was only a quarter to five when she put
her key in the door.

She shrugged off her jacket in the hallway
and stood very still, listening. Mrs. Parkhurst,
the housekeeper, was fussing around in the
kitchen, and there was a familiar rustling sound
coming from the living room. Her father, turning the pages of his evening paper. He was
home.

She wandered into the room, knowing it was
unavoidable. *Look pleasant*, she told herself.

27

Don't scowl. Present the news of the day in a relaxed but thorough manner. That's how he likes it.

"Hello, dear," he murmured, looking up from the paper. "Have a good day?"

She came over and bent slightly, presenting her cheek for the ceremonial kiss, but she jerked away as his lips approached and he hit her eyebrow instead.

"Yeah, okay," was her curt response. She went directly to the desk and opened her French grammar to start on her homework.

"Mine went well, if you're interested," he said pointedly.

She whirled around and faced him. "Oh, sorry, I should have asked. I just thought we'd talk at dinner." *Why am I apologizing?* she scolded herself.

"All right, dear," he nodded, bringing the paper back up in front of his nose. He had removed his jacket, but not his tie, and his shirtsleeves were still buttoned at the cuff. All tightly, rigidly buttoned up, as always. Becca knew, objectively, that he was a very handsome man — everyone said so, and she thought that herself, especially when she looked at old pictures of him from his medical school days in the family album. Her mother had told her that he'd gone to Europe on a trip just after his internship and had fallen in love with a beautiful Vietnamese girl he met in Paris. He had really wanted to marry her and bring her home to America, but they were from such different backgrounds that his better judgment told him she might not make the most appropriate wife for a rising young doctor. So he left her and came home. A month later he met Becca's mother on a blind date.

She stared through his newspaper, trying to see the young man who had once fallen in love with some gorgeous, exotic creature. *No, impossible*, Becca decided, turning to her homework. That was just one of her mother's romantic legends.

Mrs. Parkhurst appeared in the hallway with her coat on. "Dinner's all set, Dr. Walters," she announced in her clipped, sibilant voice. "Becca can take care of all the last-minute preparations. And I've left a casserole for tomorrow in the refrigerator."

"Very good, Mrs. Parkhurst. We'll see you Thursday morning, then, at eight-thirty sharp."

"Yes, sir," she barked. Becca knew how her father hated anyone being late, and the new housekeeper hadn't come on time once. When the front door closed with a bang, Becca cleared her throat.

"Uh, Daddy, I'm going to be getting home pretty late from now on, that is, if I get this job I've applied for. So I hope you don't mind if we eat at, like, seven or seven-thirty. Is that okay?"

Dr. Walters put his paper down. There was a very concerned expression on his face. "Would you care to tell me about the job? I didn't even know you were applying."

"Well, see, it happened sort of fast. But it's a good-paying job at the Recording for the Blind, doing sort of what I was doing in the language lab at school, only getting paid for it."

"Where is this place located? Is it in a good neighborhood?"

Becca sighed. "I . . . yes, it's right near school, as a matter of fact." She had no idea if this was the truth, but she couldn't tell him she'd never been to the place.

"And for whom would you be working?"

What was this, the Spanish Inquisition? "Oh, a really great woman — she's sort of older. One of the guys from Halsted is working for her now, and he says she's just terrific. Although a tough employer with *very* high standards," she added, knowing what would impress him. "And this guy, Mark" — she exhaled as she said his name — "he lives just a few blocks away from us, and we'd be coming home together every night. I'd be perfectly safe."

There, now you've done it. Imagined yourself a date with Mark — and you've never even said hello to him! You're a nut case, Becca!

30

"Well then, that sounds all right. I may go over and have a chat with your employer, though, to be on the safe side."

"Oh, listen, you can't . . ." She took a deep breath and nearly snapped the pencil she was holding in half.

"I can't what? What is it, dear?"

Could she tell him she was turning into a devious, manipulative, nasty liar? Could she say how she felt about his prying into her business? What would happen if she just let go, let everything come out? He'd be livid, furious! He'd probably disown her, or else monitor her every movement with one of those remote-control beeper devices he carried. *Becca Walters, turning the corner of Sixty-eighth Street, now in conversation with a person of disreputable character, now entering Baskin-Robbins for a double-dip Rocky Road cone . . .*

Yes, that was what he'd do, after he finished exploding all over the apartment. She could see it now — her father emptying like a volcano, boiling all over the carpet, the ceiling, the walls. And she herself would be carried along in the tide, no more than a puffball on the wind, rootless and insignificant.

No, she decided. It wouldn't be such a hot idea to tell him.

"Nothing." She shrugged. "It doesn't matter."

Three

Becca had mixed feelings about the job thing. She stood outside in the warm September sunshine looking at the big block letters on the side of the building: RECORDING FOR THE BLIND. They were carved in stone; they made a statement to the world. How could she offer anything to this organization, feeling as she did about herself?

Oh, don't be a nerd! she yelled silently as she turned the large brass knob and walked inside. *You know how to work machines, how to catalog tapes, how to read, for heaven's sake! You are not a helpless infant.*

But somewhere, inside, she did feel lost and alone, and it wasn't only because of the job. At least she'd convinced her father not to come with her on her first day. As she walked through the lobby to the front desk, she recalled another first, when she was eight and he'd let her walk to elementary school by herself. Well, not exactly by herself — he'd crossed Park Avenue and followed along on the opposite side of the street, signaling to her at each corner when he felt it was safe to enter the crosswalk. She'd felt so grown-up, she remembered with a smile. Today she just felt awful.

"Hello — you must be Becca." The silver-haired man behind the desk looked up over his half-glasses and gave her a fleeting smile. He had the boniest face she'd ever seen — even the bones in his temples stood out, barely covered by the mask of skin. Still, he didn't look creepy at all, just sort of absentminded. "I'm John Gormley, and officially I'm the curator here. Your supervisor will be Mrs. Samuels, the woman who interviewed you. Now, you have all your forms?"

Becca fumbled for the catch of her pocketbook and the bag slipped off her shoulder, making a loud clatter on the floor. "Oh, sorry, I —" She quickly bent to retrieve everything that had fallen. "The papers are here somewhere. It's —"

"Hey, take it easy." A voice right above her made her look up. It was Mark Shuman, and before she could stop him, he was down on his hands and knees helping her.

"Mark, maybe you'd like to show Becca around. It's not too busy right now. Just remember, the professor is coming in at five to redo that segment of his text, and he needs total supervision." The tone of Mr. Gormley's voice told Becca that he wasn't wild about the professor, whoever he was.

"Sure. Becca can watch, maybe pin the man to the floor by both shoulders if he acts up."

The two of them laughed uproariously and Becca was at a total loss. This wasn't anything like what she'd expected.

"Those forms?" Mr. Gormley prompted.

"Oh, of course. Here they are." She thrust them into his hands, and as she did so, she saw that Mark was staring at her. In her whole three years at Halsted High, she must have passed the guy a hundred times in the hall, and she'd once been in a geometry class with him. But this, she knew, was the first time he'd ever noticed she was alive. Well, she did look pretty good today, she had to admit. She'd chosen a violet cotton blouse and a plum corduroy skirt that went together perfectly. She'd managed to get her flyaway long brown hair under control with a couple of silver barrettes, and she'd even thought to put on a little pink lip gloss. Except, she thought as she watched Mr. Gormley examine her forms, Mark didn't look like the kind of guy who'd care about any of that.

"Now, whenever you get your Social Security card from that bureaucratic maze downtown, be sure and let me know your number. Can't help it — Uncle Sam insists. All right, we have no time clock here, but we do ask that you be prompt and not leave before you're supposed to."

"New kid on the block cleans up at the end of the day, too," Mark threw in smugly. "So you may be the last out of here."

"That's perfectly fine with me," Becca stated, and she meant it.

"Okay, that's about it. Mark, you start her off, and whenever Mrs. Samuels appears from the stacks again, I'll send her to your cubicle so she can say hello."

"See you later." Mark waved, and began walking down the corridor. Becca hurried after him, clutching her purse, wondering why she'd been so surprised at Judy's enthusiasm. Mark really was attractive, but he was more than that. He seemed so calm and comfortable with himself, as though he'd be able to stand in the middle of a rockslide and tell a joke if you asked him to. Becca, on the other hand, was always certain she'd be the one to start a

rockslide, and when it happened she'd be paralyzed. *Maybe I'll pick up some of his cool just
by being around him,* she thought hopefully
as he led her into a three-sided cubicle and
offered her a chair.

"You're the one Kizner sent over, right?"
he asked.

"Uh-huh."

"He says you're pretty good with recording
equipment, so I guess I won't have to teach
you too much."

"I can always stand a refresher course."
The words came out of her mouth before she
knew what she was saying. *Becca, that's awful!
You want him to think you're a flirt?* "I mean,
I'm aware there are differences in different
machinery, but I haven't used that many kinds
of recorders. Perhaps you might be able to
distinguish the variations for me." *Oh, great,
kid, now you sound about as stuffy as your
father!*

Mark looked a little puzzled, but he simply
shrugged at her nervousness. "It's not hard,
believe me. Now, I suppose you know what
Recording for the Blind is all about, but I'll
just run through it, if it won't bore you too
much."

She shook her head vehemently.

"Okay. We serve a variety of needs for the
blind or visually handicapped community. We

have master tapes of books on every subject from biophysics to business management to medicine to music composition, not to mention an awful lot of fiction. The recording studios here are used to make masters, and then, as we see what the demand is, we make copies of each tape, and those get filed in the library. Tapes are free on loan to anybody who becomes a member. And we have twenty-eight recording studios around the country to take the burden off the New York office. If a user wants a book we don't already have on file, a team of volunteer readers who know something about that subject will record it. The worst part of our job is dealing with one or two hotshots who come in here to record. You'll do a little of that yourself, and sometimes you get someone who insists he can read like Al Pacino. Like this professor who's coming in this afternoon. A real character. If I left him alone, he'd probably take all day on one sentence and try to run the machine at the same time. Most of the volunteers are really nice people, but you gotta watch out for the weirdos, okay? I'll protect you from the worst of them."

She smiled then, wondering if he'd just said that accidentally or if he really sensed how vulnerable she was. *But it's just temporary,* she told herself sternly. *I'm going to be on top of things in another week or so.*

"Sometimes we get celebs. You know, Norman Mailer or one of those diet doctors."

Becca burst out laughing.

"What's the matter?"

"Well, it's sort of funny that you put them in the same camp."

"Hey, just because someone's name is big in public circles is no reason I should get all worked up over him. It's what's inside a person — how he is with other people — that impresses me."

"I see what you mean," Becca murmured, surprised by the guy's integrity. She herself, she had to admit, was usually impressed by credentials.

Mark was talking about the procedure of doing a book on tape, and she forced her concentration back to work. Of course, it was hard not to notice his great brown eyes and those flushed cheeks, but Becca had always prided herself on being able to think about more than one thing at a time.

"So, let's take the tour." He stood up and she followed him down another corridor, where about six different sets of people were visible behind the closed doors of soundproof recording studios. It was all very professional — there were even red lights over each doorway as a cautionary measure so that no one would walk in in the middle of a recording.

"How many people work here?" she asked Mark, walking along at his side.

"Aside from Gormley and Samuels, there's me and Johnny Francone — we know a little about the mechanical side of things in case of breakdowns — and seven others like you. We're all part-time except for Johnny and the bosses. Budget cuts, you know. But we manage." He led her into a large processing room with several reel-to-reel tape machines positioned around, and then went out to the library where a nervous-looking girl with gigantic eyes and frizzed red hair was sitting behind a desk.

"Joanie, this is Becca — she's the new one," Mark said by way of introduction.

"Hi," Joanie croaked, turning bright red and looking away.

"Hello." Becca smiled. She'd never met anyone so shy. The other girl's anxiety about a simple greeting somehow made Becca feel better. *There's always somebody who needs help worse than you*, she thought with a pang of compassion for Joanie. She intended to make a point of getting to know her.

Mark walked her past the checkout desk and they proceeded down the neatly categorized stacks. He pointed out the locations of fiction, poetry, drama, how-to, biography, and children's literature and showed her how they were all in nicely color-coded tape boxes, alphabetized according to author.

"Children's lit." Becca cleared her throat.

"Yeah, that's the worst," Mark sighed, his voice taking on a totally different quality than when he'd been explaining the layout of the place. "When a mother comes in here with a blind little kid, or a whole blind class walks in with their teacher, you know, it makes you want to smash something." He shook his head and gave her a fierce look. "With all the work doctors do on cancer and heart disease and everything, you'd think they'd do a little more on some kinds of blindness. Of course, doctors generally want to do what makes them the most money, and a lot of blind people are poor."

"My father's a doctor, and he cares," Becca insisted.

"Oh? What's his field?"

"He's a general practitioner, mostly gastrointestinal."

"I see, a lot of rich old ladies."

"That's not true! He works in a clinic every other afternoon," she retorted hotly.

"Becca, Becca! Hold on." Mark suddenly reached for her hand. "I'm not indicting your father for criminal misconduct. I was just making a generalization."

"Yeah," she said, thinking she ought to pull away but not doing it. "Well, don't."

He grinned at her and didn't say anything for a minute. Then he said softly, "I honestly didn't mean anything by it. One of these evenings after work I'll buy you a Coke to show you I'm not such a bad guy, okay?"

Was he asking her for a date? *Oh, you're such a dummy*, she thought critically when he didn't wait for a response but began pulling her along the row until they came out right in front of the main listening area. *You always take everything so seriously*. That wasn't an invitation; it was just a thing to say. For all intents and purposes they had only just met, and no one asked for a date after one half hour of talking. *It's only that you're so stuck on yourself you think everyone else is, too.*

But as she trailed along beside Mark, it also occurred to her that if they started going out and things were awful or awkward, then they'd break up and they'd still have to see each other every day at work or at school. At least her mother was in Michigan and would never have to see her father again if she didn't want to. Oh, it was ridiculous, really, to be thinking this way!

Becca, stop it! she commanded herself. But she couldn't.

They were now standing in the main listening area, a maze of little open cubicles with recording machines and headphones in each one.

"I don't really have to tell you about these — they're the same as in the language lab. Now, we all take turns in every area — assisting with recording, cataloging new tapes and filing ones that have been returned, working the library desk where Joanie was sitting, and then there's the checkout counter. The schedule board is in Samuels's office. Hey, we better bring you in to see her before the professor comes, or else she's going to start thinking we've eloped."

Becca's stomach bunched up in a knot. He sure honed right in on her sensitive spots. Eloping made her think of marriage and marriage naturally made her think of her parents. Any notion of her parents' marriage led directly, without passing GO, to her parents' divorce.

Mark was walking her briskly down the back corridor, and as he turned to say something, he caught a glimpse of the pained expression on her face. "Are you okay?" he asked curiously.

"Me? Oh, sure, of course, why wouldn't I be?" She laughed nervously. "It's just . . . oh, a new job and all this stuff to learn."

"I'll help you," he said simply.

The rest of the afternoon went swiftly, from

the conference with Mrs. Samuels ("Remember, organization is primary in our work here") to the recording sessions with Professor Stanislav Romboff, who was, as Mark had warned her, a real character. He was obviously concerned about having a good retake of Chapter Twelve of *A Modern Interpretation of Ancient Ideas* and would have insisted that they keep doing it over all evening long had Becca not been able to charm him with the little white lie: "It was just perfect that time, professor."

"Gee, I was never able to convince anyone that stubborn," Mark commented when they were putting on their jackets at six-ten.

"Well, sometimes I have a way with the stuffy, being as how I'm somewhat stuffy myself." Becca smiled, a bit embarrassed by his praise.

"You? Never!" Mark snatched up her book bag with his. "I think personally it was more like witchcraft, you know." He rolled his eyes and she looked away, completely flustered. She was rooted to the spot.

"Let's go or they'll lock us in." Mark hurried her along to the front door. The moment felt good, even though it made her very anxious.

"So, guess I'll see you tomorrow," Mark smiled, letting his jacket drape casually around his shoulders. "This is my subway," he added, jerking his thumb in the direction of the IRT.

"Oh, yeah, well, I'll see you." Becca turned and started walking up Sixty-eighth Street, wishing she could just have said, "It's my subway, too," which it was. But that would look like she was tagging along after him. She certainly didn't want to spoil anything, and the only alternative was to take the bus. Her father had supplied her with an extra five-dollar bill for a cab, saying that she couldn't be too careful, now that she was coming home late, but she decided against it. The bus would take longer, anyway.

She put her key in the lock and held her breath, summoning her strength and her good feelings about Mark to carry her through the evening with her father. It was just such a downer to come home to this! But when she turned the knob, she was surprised to find that the hallway was dark, as was the rest of the apartment.

"Hello?" Her voice echoed around her.

She flipped on the lights, and her eye immediately went to the phone on the hall table. A piece of yellow legal paper had been tucked into the dial. In her father's meticulous hand was written:

Darling,

*Mr. Pierpont in Brooklyn went into
cardiac arrest this afternoon, so I had
to go down there and admit him to the
hospital. His wife is quite upset, so
I may be a while. Eat dinner without
me — I should be home by 8:30.*
                    Daddy

Becca sighed. Naturally, she felt sorry about
the poor patient, but reading this note brought
back memories of so many notes like it over
the years, and her mother's outrageous reaction to them. Heart attacks were an everyday
affair for a general practitioner. When Rachel
read about the fifth coronary in as many weeks,
she would invariably shrug at Becca and say,
"They're just dropping off like flies." Becca
thought her mother was terrible to even think
such things, but secretly she thought it was
kind of funny.

She read the note again and frowned when
she came to the end. Why did her father still
insist that she call him "Daddy"? It was so
babyish and it sounded odd to Becca whenever she said it. But how could you change the
pattern of sixteen years? She imagined herself
confronting her father at the door with his
note. "I think it best, now that Rachel's gone,
that we address each other as equals, David,"

she'd say. Oh, yuk, he'd never go for that. Well, how about "Dad"? It was a good clean word, very American in tone. Becca shook her head and carried the note into the kitchen. Two stuffy people like her and her father should call each other "Ms. Walters" and "Dr. Walters." But she wasn't stuffy! Mark had said she had witchcraft, for heaven's sake!

"Okay, Pop," she said to the thin air. "From now on, I'd like you to call me Witchy."

She opened the refrigerator and peered inside. Mrs. Parkhurst had left them breaded pork chops and broiled tomato halves to heat and serve.

"I'm not really that hungry," Becca said aloud. "Maybe I'll just snack." There was a lot of fruit and an opened package of Jarlsberg cheese as well as assorted leftovers, none of which looked terribly appetizing. Becca sighed and took a Tab off the top shelf before slamming the door.

" 'Stay me with flagons, comfort me with apples/For I am sick of love,' " she sighed theatrically, popping open her soda.

Love. That was an odd word. It even looked odd when you wrote it down. Such a short word, so inconsequential, really. Four little letters that meant a whole world. Becca smiled, thinking that *Mark* was another dynamite four-letter word. He was so — how could she put it? — he looked like somebody surrounded by

46

friends and family. He probably had five brothers and three sisters. A house with lots of laughter. Yes, he was definitely the kind of guy who'd never had to eat dinner alone in his life.

Becca hurt inside when she remembered the days of family meals, the three of them seated at the table, sharing the news of the day. Of course, her parents had always kept the conversation trained on Becca so they could avoid talking to each other, but still, dinnertime had always had a semblance of warm family feeling to it. Her mother was no great shakes as a cook, but there was usually some little treat to make the meal an occasion. Becca was the only kid in third grade ever to bring cream cheese and caviar sandwiches in her lunchbox. It was only red lumpfish, left over from a party the night before, but it certainly made her a celebrity at school. Especially because it was topped off with some of her mother's homemade tollhouse cookies. They were the only item in Rachel's baking repertoire, but they were delicious, and the warm perfume of those cookies, hot out of the oven, was enough to make the whole house smell like home.

"That's it!" Becca laughed aloud, snapping her fingers. "I'll bake him a cake. Something gooey and sinful." She got out the stepladder and clambered up to the shelf that held five rather dusty cookbooks. If they had the right ingredients on hand, she could create a genuine masterpiece for her father, and that would take his mind off the variety of critical comments that formed in his brain the instant he laid eyes on her. A successful dessert, just for him, would show him she was really trying, and that she wanted things to be good between them.

She scanned the first book, *The Joy of Cooking*, and put it aside as too commonplace. The next, *Royal Treats of Morocco*, which her mother had bought because of one recipe she'd read in *The New York Times*, was clearly wrong for the occasion. The next was Julia Child, *Mastering the Art of French Cooking*.

"Perfect!" Becca exclaimed, opening to the dessert and cake section. She adored watching Julia Child on television, throwing things around the kitchen in what looked like total confusion, and always ending up with a perfect product. The chocolate and almond cake sounded fantastic, but where was she going to get pulverized almonds at this hour? So she picked the orange sponge cake with orange butter-cream icing.

"He'll love this!" she declared, scrounging through shelves and cabinets for the ingredients. She could even bring a piece to Mark at work. Wouldn't he be surprised? "I always thought of you as a pure intellectual," he'd say, "and now I find you can cook, too!"

First, Julia instructed, she was to separate four eggs. Becca took the first one from the carton and cracked it on the side of the bowl. Quickly, she inverted one half and let the white slide out; then, like a magician doing a sleight of hand, she flipped the yolk to the other half. Terrific! The round yellow globe was still intact. After a couple more flips, she was satisfied that she had all the white, and she dumped the yolk in the second bowl.

"Only three to go," she assured herself calmly. Unfortunately, these did not go as well. One yolk ran into the whites and another dropped on the counter before she could salvage any of it. The third had only a very small yolk, so she did two more to be on the safe side. Her mixture of whites looked awfully yellow, but as she glanced up at the clock and saw it was almost eight, she hurried on.

The next chore was beating the sugar into the yolks until it formed a ribbon. Becca wasn't sure that her "ribbon" was anything like Julia's, but she persevered, adding orange juice, grated orange peel — sort of flakes instead of grates — salt, and flour. In her haste to get the cake into the oven, she jerked her hand and most of the flour spilled all over the counter. She dumped in another half cup or so, but the consistency still seemed sort of funny.

"Oh, well," she sighed, going on to the egg whites. She beat them until her arm was tired, but the stupid things wouldn't form peaks. The egg yolks streaked through made the whole thing heavy and impossible. "You're just like my mood these days," she muttered to the ingredients.

Becca sighed and started to blend the whites and the batter. Julia said to stir some in and delicately fold in the rest, but by the time Becca had combined the contents of both bowls, everything was pretty well stirred in. "You better rise," she threatened the cake as she poured it into the greased pan and walked it to the oven.

She'd forgotten to preheat it! Quickly, she lit the oven and turned the thermometer to 500 degrees. Julia said to bake it at 350 degrees, but maybe you could turn the heat down after you preheated. She set her timer for thirty minutes and started on the orange-butter filling, slightly anxious about what her finished product was going to look like.

About halfway through the cooking process, she smelled something. She grabbed a pot-holder and whipped open the oven door. There, in a small sizzling lump, was an acrid burnt-orange cake, less than halfway up the side of the pan. The edges were black and the center was a liquid pool of egg and crystallized sugar.

"Oh, no!" Becca wailed, and just then she heard the front door open. The clock on the wall read eight-fifteen. Doom time.

"What the . . . ?" She heard her father's voice in the hall. "What do I smell? Becca, where are you?"

"In here." She willed herself to be calm, but she couldn't stop the tears. Two jagged tracks cut through her flour-dusted face.

Dr. Walters stormed into the kitchen, took one look at his daughter, and lurched over to open the window. "You could have set the place on fire!" His mustache bristled with anger, and his eyebrows were raised so high they looked like they might jump into his scalp at any moment. Becca was quivering with rage at her own incompetence. Here it was — yet another job messed up, yet another thing for him to criticize.

"Well, the smoke alarm didn't go off, so I guess we're okay," she sniffled, wanting to seem in control instead of being just a puddle on the floor. "I was baking you a cake," she added in a choked voice.

Her father blinked once and took a step backward, as though he'd been hit. Then something in his face changed and softened. "What kind of cake was it?" he asked after a moment.

"Julia Child. It had a lot of eggs and orange juice. You probably wouldn't have liked it, anyway," she shrugged, wiping a cheek with the back of her sticky hand.

"Orange is always nice," he murmured, taking the potholder from the counter and going over to examine the cake more carefully. "But maybe tomorrow we ought to try chocolate."

"Huh?" Becca was still waiting for the explosion.

"How about a trip to the supermarket? We could look around, see what we're partial to, then come home and cook it."

"You mean . . . you want to cook?" Becca wondered what was the matter with him. Probably he was so relieved she hadn't set the house on fire that he'd become slightly loony. That was just temporary, of course.

"I cooked in my fraternity house in college, you know," he reminded her, taking a knife from the rack and chopping up the mess in the baking pan before dumping it in the garbage. "I wasn't all that bad. But you'll have to give me some pointers about cake baking."

Becca's puzzled frown slowly smoothed into a grin. "I think we'll both have to call Julia Child and get some advice from her. I seem to be about the world's worst cake baker."

"Nonsense," her father barked abruptly. "So, is it a date? Shopping first; cooking afterward. I'll be home about six tomorrow."

Becca felt a weird sensation start somewhere in the area of her stomach. Probably just hunger pangs. "Sure," she nodded.

"I suppose we should have some supper — why don't we go out for a hamburger," he said on his way out of the kitchen.

Becca's brain wasn't functioning too well, but she did manage to remember where her father had been for the past few hours. "How's Mr. Pierpont?" she asked.

"He'll live," was Dr. Walters's response.

*F*our

The next afternoon flew by. Between Mrs. Samuels's carefully written instructions and Mark's helpful presence, Becca had no time to think about anything but adjusting to her new job. But at five-thirty, she suddenly began anticipating the evening to come. Suppose her father was only interested in buying frozen fish in plastic envelopes and broccoli spears smothered in Velveeta cheese? Should she protest, or do whatever he wanted? She could just hear her mother now. "Don't argue with him, Becca. He's the boss, right?"

Becca had never really agreed. As she packed her things to leave work, she thought about the phone conversation she'd had with her mother two nights ago. Things were great in Michigan, school was "nifty," whatever that meant. Rachel had never asked how Becca was doing in her new life, but she'd sure been curious about her soon-to-be ex-husband. "How does he look? Is he eating and everything?" she'd asked nervously. "He's fine," Becca had answered noncommittally. Her mother really could be annoying at times.

"Which way are you going?" Mark was standing right behind her, and she jumped when she heard his voice. "Sorry, didn't see you were daydreaming," he teased.

"I wasn't!" she lied.

"Want to go get a Coke?" he asked, swinging his gray-blue muffler around the collar of his leather bomber jacket.

"Uh, I can't *tonight*." She stressed the final word. Oh, this was so typical. He would pick the exact night she couldn't go. "I promised my father I'd help him go shopping. But maybe some other time," she added hopefully as they walked out the door and down the front steps of the building.

"Yeah, well, my limo awaits me." He turned in the direction of the IRT.

"I'm in a rush tonight, so I guess I'll take

the train, too," she said nervously, walking briskly after him. Mark turned to look at her in the dim evening light, and she could see the puzzled expression on his face.

"You live uptown?" he asked.

"East eighties." She fumbled in her bag for her change purse so she'd be sure to have her token ready by the time they were down the stairs of the subway.

"Then how do you usually go home?" he quizzed her as they walked past the token booth.

"Oh, you know, walking, or I take the bus. Sometimes the subway." She knew she didn't sound casual, hard as she was trying.

"Well, in the future" — Mark smiled, ushering her through the turnstile — "let me know. I'll go whichever way you want."

"Oh, okay," Becca said as evenly as she could.

The platform was filling up, and Mark grabbed her hand to lead her along the scuzzy, littered walkway to the end of the train. The smell of rotten banana was overpowering.

"Dontcha love it? New York's a trip, isn't it?" he yelled over the racket of the local careening into the station.

"I've never lived anywhere else," she screamed back.

"I spent a summer in New Hampshire once,"

he told her as he jockeyed for space to get them inside the one functioning door of their car. "Worst time I ever had. Man, you could hear the birds laying their eggs! It was that quiet. And nothing — no excitement, no bagels, and one movie theater with second-run films that ran for a whole week apiece!"

"Sounds pretty terrible," Becca giggled.

"Yeah, my lungs even got clean that summer. It was a horrible shock." The train gave a lurch, and they were thrown smack against one another.

"Oh, sorry." Becca pulled back quickly, but she wasn't sorry at all.

"You know, that's an idea," Mark nodded. "How about a movie this weekend?"

"You mean a . . . ?"

"There's a lot of things on my 'must see' list. You like foreign films or domestic?"

"Oh, both." *Becca, don't waffle. Say something intelligent.* "I read a great review of that new Australian film in the *Voice*."

"Say, I saw that, too! And I really like the guy's earlier work. So I'll call for the times it goes on, okay? Is Saturday better for you, or Sunday?"

"Uh, Saturday would be fine." Becca's eyes saw through the myriad numbers of people surrounding them to the clear possibility — no, probability! — of a date. A real date!

"Okay. See you tomorrow. This is my stop."

Then he was gone. Becca rode on to Eighty-sixth Street with a gigantic grin plastered across her face. The grungy subway had metamorphosed into a coach, driven by four snow-white horses and she, Becca Walters, in a puff of smoke, had turned into Cinderella dressed for the ball.

Her father was seated at the dining room table when she walked in, his jacket and tie in place, a notebook and a pencil neatly laid before him.

"Hello, dear, how was your day?" He turned and smiled at her absentmindedly. "I was just making this list."

You would, Becca thought, but she pulled up a chair beside him.

"Did you check the refrigerator?"

"Yes. We appear to be out of almost everything — and maybe it would be a good idea to stock up on dry and canned goods while we're at it."

Becca could picture her father stockpiling food and provisions, filling every corner of the apartment with cases of tuna fish and toilet paper. "Now we're settling in," he'd say, locking and barring the door.

She snapped out of her reverie long enough to add a couple of items to the list that he'd missed. He shook his head in shame. "I have to tell you, Becca, that I haven't been inside a supermarket in, well, I don't want to count the years. I'm afraid I was one of those unliberated men who got married and just sat up and begged for my supper."

Becca bit her lip. Did she dare to make a joke? "Good thing you didn't sing for it."

"You said it!" He roared with laughter and Becca's mouth dropped open. He led the way into the hall, and she rang for the elevator while he locked up.

"Do you know what you'd like for dinner tonight? This has to be a special meal, you know," he insisted, his dark brown eyes sparkling with amusement.

"Maybe we should just look around and see what appeals to us," Becca suggested. They walked out of the building and down Eighty-fourth Street to Lexington Avenue.

"Good idea." The light turned green and a taxi screeched to a halt in front of them. Her father's arm shot out and pulled her back. "Damn idiot! Why don't they take licenses away from people like that?" He pounded on the hood of the car once before yanking her across the street.

Oh, great. Now he's off and running. All her father needed was one bone of contention to chew on and it could spoil a whole evening.

Becca could clearly remember times from her childhood when some little tiny thing would go wrong and he'd spend the rest of the evening berating her mother every time she took a breath.

Well, I'm going to act like an adult and set an example for him, Becca decided as they stepped on the mat that controlled the supermarket's automatic door. After all, she felt very good about herself tonight. She had just been asked out on a date for Saturday!

Oh, boy, wait'll I tell him that. "Who is the young man, Becca? Where does he live? What do his parents do? Will he grow up to be President of the United States?" Yuk.

"Here, dear, you take the list, and I'll push the cart around." He tried unsuccessfully to pry one cart from the others in front of it. Becca let him struggle for a few seconds before lightly lifting the cart and giving it a sharp jerk away.

"Oh, I see, that's how it's done. Thank you, dear."

Five points for Becca; penalty for Dr. Walters.

The first aisle was condiments and salad dressings. They chose a jar of French mustard and three different dressings, and then Becca ran over and picked up some jumbo black olives.

"Excellent idea!" her father nodded, blinking a bit from the bright neon and the assortment of colored product labels. It was true, Becca thought, watching him examine one item after the other. If you weren't used to it, a supermarket could be a pretty crazy place.

The next aisle was baking products. "Maybe we should try a packaged cake mix instead of Julia, what do you say?" her father suggested, picking up a box with a gigantic chocolate layer cake on it.

"Daddy, have you ever read the ingredients on one of these things?" Becca asked her doctor father in a shocked voice. "There's barely a speck of naturalness in it — total chemicals." She made a face and took the box away from him.

"Hmm. I guess so," he murmured, pushing on to the cereal display. "Well, we do need some cornflakes . . . will you look at this!" He began chuckling as he picked up a few boxes. "Count Chocula! Who eats these things? Cap'n Crunch! I had no idea there were so many different ones. Say, we could probably make a phenomenal dessert out of the cake mix and some of this stuff." He shook the box and listened to it. "Just add water and serve."

Becca giggled. This wasn't so bad after all. And her father really seemed to be getting a kick out of it. She grabbed a box of Raisin Bran — "just for a change of pace, Daddy," — and then led him to the aisle filled with rice and tomato products. Her father was astounded at all the "helper" items and rice concoctions with envelopes of seasoning.

"Don't people cook from scratch anymore?" he asked in a worried tone. "You know, this is what's wrong with America. Nobody cares."

"We never used to eat this junk," Becca informed him, picking up a package of plain long-grain rice. "Mom was pretty enthusiastic about healthy eating, if you recall."

"Was she? I never noticed," he murmured, pushing the cart ahead quickly. "What about, let's see, a really good Italian meat sauce." He scanned the shelves. "I don't think that should be too hard. Just tomatoes and paste and garlic — lots of garlic. I'll be the hit of the hospital tomorrow."

Becca grinned at him. "Garlic keeps werewolves away, too."

"That's vampires, darling. Don't you know anything!"

And then, in the middle of the crowded supermarket, they looked at each other and started laughing hysterically. Becca was suddenly all warm inside, filled to bursting with affection for this man. Most of the time, he might seem stiff and stern and as uncomfortable as a Victorian gentleman stuck in a crowd of punk-rockers, but when he didn't try so hard to be a paragon of social perfection, he was really a lot of fun. And then she realized that he actually liked spending time with her. Becca had never known that before.

"Well," she said thoughtfully, throwing several cans of tomatoes into the cart, "Italian spaghetti seems like a project for a long weekend. Maybe we should be less ambitious tonight."

"Yes, I suppose you're right. What about a meat loaf?"

"Great! You can throw all sorts of things in there," Becca enthused, leading him around to the meat counter. "A box of Soup Starter, then some Hamburger Helper, and we could top the whole thing off with a Pop Tart."

"A what?"

"Oh, you'd love them, Daddy. They're sort of shaped like a playing card and they've got jam in the middle. You stick them in the toaster and heat them up. Very convenient."

Her father shook his head and scanned their shopping list again. "Let's be a little more conservative with *this* meat loaf, all right? Next time we can be experimental." The words were typical David Walters, and yet, Becca sensed something very different about them. It was as if he was making fun of himself! Not that he didn't still believe all his maxims and axioms, but tonight he seemed to be able to see around his blinders.

Funny, Becca thought as they cruised the aisles for vegetables and bread crumbs. *When I was a kid, we never would have thought of doing something like this together. It was me and Mom, Mom and me, with him on the outside like the wrapping on a package. He must have felt pretty neglected. Nothing like Mark as a kid, I bet, with hundreds of brothers and sisters and friends and good times.*

She stopped herself suddenly. Why was she thinking about Mark? It made her feel funny to think of Mark and her father in the same moment. Anyhow, they were nothing alike.

It was easier now to see her father as the little boy he must have been, not really popular, never being asked to play on a team or anything because he seemed so aloof. *Or did he just get that way after he married Mom, as a defense?*

"Now, what about dessert?" Her father's cheery tone roused her from the daydream. "You've ruled out the evil cake mix, so we need a substitute. Do you want a nice fruit salad?"

Becca wrinkled up her nose. "Say, let's have a party. You can't have a party without ice cream." She made a beeline for the frozen food section and stood in front of the ice cream freezer, debating. "What's your favorite flavor?" It was strange, but she'd never noticed that her father was more partial to one than to another. For a man with preferences so strong they were virtually unchangeable, that seemed odd. Probably ice cream was too frivolous to make decisions about.

"I don't really care, dear. You pick."

She chose a pint of mocha almond and one of chocolate chip. Then they made a final circuit of the market, just in case they'd forgotten anything. They arrived at the checkout counter barely able to see over the top of their cart.

"Oh, no," her father moaned. "How are we going to get this all home?"

Becca looked at her father curiously. He sure was inexperienced about certain things. "They deliver, Daddy. How do you think Mrs. Parkhurst does it?"

"Oh . . . oh, yes, of course," he said quickly, rather embarrassed for not seeing this possibility.

"But since we want to get started on dinner, why don't we just keep out the stuff we'll need and take it with us?"

Her father's face lit up. It was as if she'd just presented him with a new way to split the atom. "You're a very clever girl," he nodded, withdrawing his wallet from his pocket. "I don't know what I'd do without you."

Becca stood there holding a jar of olives in one hand and a roll of paper towels in the other. She wanted so badly to hug him. But it would have looked pretty silly, right there at the checkout counter, to embrace your father, so she just smiled and kept unloading.

They carried their two bags into the kitchen and Becca lit the oven to preheat it, not wanting a repeat of last night's fiasco.

"Now, where do we start?" Her father removed his jacket and placed it carefully over a kitchen chair. Then he unbuttoned his cuffs and rolled up his sleeves before going to the sink to wash his hands. Becca noticed that he took off his watch and his wedding ring so they wouldn't get wet. He was still wearing his ring! Did that mean . . . ? Her heart started pounding. It was so loud, she was sure he could hear it across the kitchen. *Oh, just cool it*, she told herself, turning to unpack some of the groceries. *It's over, kid. He just wears the ring because old habits die hard — especially with him.*

"I think I'll put some Worcestershire sauce in and a lot of basil. You chop up an onion, dear, and throw an egg in." He was already breaking up the meat into a bowl Becca had put in front of him.

"Peas and carrots for a vegetable?" she asked, holding the frozen package up for his inspection.

"That sounds good. Now, I remember one time up in Canada where I did my internship. I had this apartment — well, it was actually a hole in the wall. You see, the landlady was such a tightfisted woman, she'd had her cousin divide one floor of their house into three apartments, so she could have three tenants and collect three rents."

"Really?" Becca watched her father's face become animated as he reminisced. He hardly ever talked about his past. *Boy, maybe I can get him to talk about the Vietnamese girl.* She felt slightly guilty, as though she were betraying her mother, but she was really curious.

"Yes, well, naturally I had no kitchen and there was just one bath down the hall for all of us. The worst part of it was that this landlady kept the heat down as low as she could tolerate it to save money, and we were obliged to go around bundled up in layers of clothing. But the point of this story, Becca" — he took the cutting board filled with the chopped onion and dumped it all into the bowl — "is that I was not too well off financially, so I couldn't eat out in restaurants all the time. I got myself a little hotplate, and I used to cook up some very creditable meals, I must say."

"You taught yourself?" She put the vegetables in a pot and set the cover on them.

"Well, it was very much like chemistry. A

little of this and that, and I just fiddled around until the mixture seemed right. I did eggs of all varieties, and omelets, and I was quite good with chicken. I tried to accustom my palate to the least expensive foods — kidneys, liver, that sort of thing — but I guess I was just a gourmet at heart."

"I never knew you cooked, Daddy," she murmured as she took the bowl from him and added a drop of milk. Then she put both her hands into the meat loaf mix and worked everything in together.

"Certainly I did. Although I have to confess I was a lot happier when I started my residency in New York and was making enough money to have someone do it for me."

Someone. That was Rachel. She was a lousy cook, though. Becca wondered why her father hadn't done the cooking and let her mother be the fixit person, since she did that better. *I guess people weren't so liberated in those days*, Becca mused, turning the meat into a Pyrex dish and setting it in the oven. Everyone had his or her role, and if they didn't play it right they got the ax. Becca had this mental image of her mother wearing an apron and holding a pot, standing up on a stage while a whole audience full of David Walterses booed her into the wings. Pretty sad, when you thought about it.

"Now" — her father set the timer for forty-five minutes — "we can watch the news or read the paper. Or you might tackle some of that homework. What do you say?" He washed his hands again, and then he rolled down his cuffs and buttoned them.

"Daddy, we're having a party, remember? Homework is for later. Say, I know! What about a little music before dinner? That would be so civilized. Just like one of those fancy restaurants where the gypsy violinist comes to your table and plays sobbing melodies right in your ear."

Without waiting for his approval, she raced into the living room and grabbed her violin case. She took the instrument lovingly from its felt bed and plucked the strings. As her father took his seat in his chair, a contented smile on his face, she began tuning up.

"Let's see, for our first number of the evening," she announced, flipping her hair over her opposite shoulder as she always did before playing, "we will have an original piece by Becca Walters." She drew the bow dramatically over the strings in a sort of fanfare. "Did I tell you I'm working on some composing? Ms. Claymore says it's a waste of time, but I told her I'm never going to be a concert performer, so I may as well write music."

The doctor crossed his legs and looked at

her intently. "Now dear, if she says you're wasting your time —"

"Oh, Daddy, come on. Okay, so here's how it goes. Uh, that is, if I remember." She laughed. She cleared her throat and started, but no sooner had she played eight bars of the piece than she drew a blank. *Damn!* It was like a prophecy. She'd said it, and sure enough, she'd forgotten. With a sigh, she put her bow down.

"Oh, phooey, let's have some olives." She took the violin from her shoulder.

"Did you write the music down? Why don't you get it out and read it properly?"

She groaned softly under her breath and stared at her father. "Daddy," she muttered, "this isn't Carnegie Hall, you know. I was just fooling around."

"Darling, no one ever succeeded by fooling around."

She bit her lip, crushed inside. "I know that. Look, I'll practice after dinner. After my homework, okay? Will that please you?"

"It isn't a question of pleasing me, Becca, it's —"

"Right." She laid the instrument on the felt and smartly closed the lid, snapping the two locks shut. She couldn't look at him. "Maybe later. I don't feel like it now. I guess I'll go set the table." She left the violin sitting on the desk and turned on her heel, knowing that if she was ever going to grow up, she would have to tell him what she thought and not feel like she'd just started World War III all by herself.

As soon as she stepped across the threshold into the dining room, she heard his footsteps behind her. "I'll help you," he said in a quiet voice, and when she turned around, she saw to her surprise that he wasn't angry. As a matter of fact, if her father had ever been close to an apology in his life, it looked like he was right now.

"Tablecloth or mats?" she asked, going to the sideboard. Her mother had even polished the silver before she left, Becca noted as she opened the chest and the utensils gleamed up at her. *My mother was nuts!* She suddenly understood. By never talking back to her father, by giving in and insisting that he was always right and she was always wrong, Rachel had only succeeded in breeding an awful lot of contempt. *I just defied him and things are okay now. Maybe that's more normal.*

"I like these," her father smiled, picking up some gaily flowered placemats. "They remind me of spring, you know?"

"Uh-huh." There *was* something different about him tonight. He seemed more open and willing to accept things. She came over to him with the silverware, and for a moment they stood right next to each other. Becca could smell the nice combination of his after-shave

and the crisp Band-Aid odor she always asso-
ciated with his office. She closed her eyes, re-
membering nights when her parents would
come in late from a party and tiptoe into her
room to kiss her good night. She had always
pretended she was sleeping, hoping to catch a
whisper of love between Rachel and David.

Love. There was that word again. Love was
supposed to make marriages work, it was supposed to heal up all the open sores. Just fleet-
ingly, she wondered what it took to really fall
in love, the kind that was for keeps. And then,
just briefly, she thought of Mark again. Of
course, she hardly knew him — hadn't even
gone out on a date with him yet — but he
seemed like the kind of person who wouldn't
take the word *love* lightly.

Unlike her parents.

Poor people, she thought, putting a fork,
knife, and spoon at the two lonely place settings. *They never were able to give each other
what they needed.*

"That looks nice." Her father crossed his
arms and stared at the rather bare table. "Maybe we should get some sort of centerpiece —
a bowl or something — to liven it up a little.
You look around for something the next time
you're in Bloomingdale's, all right?"

"Oh, wait." In a spontaneous whirl, she
raced to the closet and began rummaging
around. "I know exactly what we need." At

last her hand found the flat box. "This is so perfect!" she enthused, removing candles and candlesticks from their partitions and setting them carefully in the middle of the table. "Atmosphere is so important at a formal dinner, don't you agree?" she giggled, turning to her father with an impish look of delight. "We'll dim the lights and —"

She stopped at once, seeing his face. His whole attitude had changed in that brief instant. Shoulders slumped, he stood staring at her offering, a look of terrible sadness enveloping him.

Oh, what have I done? Becca agonized. *What did I say? Everything was so good up till now.* Hundreds of possibilities flashed through her mind, each one less plausible than the next, until finally a picture of Rachel formed in her mind. She was lighting candles for "an intimate, romantic meal," as she always called it.

Boy, are you dumb! Becca whisked the offensive reminders off the table and shoved them into a drawer of the sideboard. Her face felt flushed, as though she'd just opened a hot oven and peered inside.

"Maybe I'll check on the meat loaf," she murmured, hastening into the kitchen. She could no longer look at her father's ravaged face. He seemed so lost, so much more alone than Becca was herself, that suddenly she felt terribly guilty. She'd been selfish, and she'd never considered his problems. It couldn't be easy for him, dealing with a teenage daughter all by himself, especially one he hardly knew.

She stirred the peas and carrots and poured some fat off the nearly cooked meat loaf, trying to think of something cheery to say, something that would make him know she didn't want them to be strangers anymore.

Taking a deep breath, she pushed open the kitchen door. Her father was seated at the table, his head in his hands.

"Uh . . . what do you want to drink?" *Well, go on, say something*. She wanted to so badly.

They ate in silence, and Becca found each bite of food as hard to swallow as her realization that her father was a difficult person to get to know. Would they ever be close? she wondered mournfully. Then she pushed her chair back and got up to bring in dessert.

Five

"I still can't believe it!" Judy was sitting beside Becca in the kitchen of the Sterns' large West Side apartment. "A date with Mark Shuman tonight — and you don't look the least bit excited." Judy was over her crush on Mark and on to someone else, so Becca's date didn't bother her.

"Now stop that, Stephi." Mrs. Stern paraded through the kitchen carrying an overloaded laundry hamper while the youngest Stern, an adorable eight-year-old with Judy's eyes, waved a bubble wand in the air. "You're going to use up all my liquid detergent."

"They're so pretty, Ma! Much better than the gunk in the bottle. This is blue, see?" Stephi offered the measuring cup of detergent to Becca for her inspection.

"Ma!" Deborah Stern wandered into the kitchen, her radio turned up to full volume so that The Who's "You Better" blasted out any conversation. "I can't find my peach blouse anywhere."

"That's because I'm washing it, dear. Oh, nice to see you, Becca," Mrs. Stern added over her shoulder.

Becca loved being here. The Stern house was always lively, full of movement and noise and people. So unlike her own mausoleum on the opposite side of town. Sterns seemed to pop out of nowhere, arguing or singing or doing chores. The way this family lived and worked together made Becca feel really out of it, like she'd just been sent down from a desolate moon colony to observe the habits of humans. But it was good being a part of the action — the Sterns always tried to include her. She felt alive in this house, like a deaf person suddenly able to hear for the first time. *This is what family means,* she told herself, pushing away the plate of cookies in front of her. She felt really queasy, and had since she woke up that morning. It wasn't a constant thing, but every once in a while a wave of nausea would hit her. Probably the fried clams she'd grabbed for lunch the day before. But she was sure the feeling would go away by evening if she didn't eat anything.

"Becca, stop dreaming," Judy grumbled, getting up to turn off her older sister's radio. Deborah waited until Judy took her seat again, and then she turned it right back on.

"I have to hear this, for heaven's sake," she yelled as she stalked out of the room.

"Now tell me, what are you wearing?" Judy asked as she fended off Stephi's bubbles, which the little girl was blowing all over them.

"I don't know. I guess cords and a nice shirt."

"You're so calm and bloodless. Get enthusiastic, will you?" Judy said impatiently.

"Well, I am, honest, it's just that I'm feeling a little under the weather, that's all," Becca said weakly.

"Believe me, once you see Mark, arriving at your front door all shiny and polished for the evening, you'll feel like a million. What are you seeing, a Japanese film?"

"Australian. He's a real film buff, you know."

"No, I didn't know. He doesn't talk to lowly me, dearheart. Boy, were you ever smart to get that job at that recording place. Stuck there hour after hour, filing those tapes down dark, romantic corridors . . ." Judy fantasized.

"Judy! You're as bad as my mother! It's just a job, not a Hollywood contract."

Judy pushed her little sister out of the way and gathered up the dishes from the table. "Well, maybe, but it sure seems glamorous."

Becca was suddenly seized with a stomach-gripping cramp, and she clamped her lips together in discomfort. " 'Scuse me for a second," she said, lurching toward the bathroom. But as soon as she got there, she was fine again.

"Hey, you don't look so hot. Sit down, I'll get you some club soda," Judy said with concern.

"That would be great, thanks," Becca sighed, easing herself back into the seat. "I'd really hate to have to cancel tonight."

"Cancel! Are you out of your mind? You can't turn Mark down. You know what that does to a guy's ego? I mean, he'd be totally devastated. You can't!"

Becca grimaced. "Where'd you get all this stuff, out of Deborah's psych textbook?"

"Becca, I just know it. Trust me, you say no to him this once and he'll never ask you out again. Remember me and Tom Binehart last summer?" She clucked her tongue at her own tactical error.

"Yes, but —"

"No buts! Now go home and lie down for an hour or so. Have some more club soda." She pushed the glass back into Becca's hand.

"Maybe your father can give you something."

"Ha!" Becca said, easing herself out of her chair. "My father is the original no-drugs doctor. I have to be practically dying to get an aspirin. 'Bye, Mrs. Stern," she called into the laundry room. " 'Bye, Steph." She patted the bubble-blower on the head.

"You feel good, Becky," said Stephi.

Once out in the cold air on Broadway, Becca felt better. She started walking downtown to the Eighty-sixth Street crosstown bus, slowly meandering from one shop window to the next, examining the brilliant display of fruits and vegetables on the many Korean stands along the way. This neighborhood was so great — the kids, the shopping bag ladies, the beautifully dressed couples spilling out of chic restaurants. The upper West Side was the flip side of the stuffy poshness of Becca's neighborhood. Everybody seemed to be embalmed once you crossed Central Park. *Even me*, she thought ruefully.

She stopped to buy some crisp green and red apples, thinking the fruit might be all she'd be able to get down before her date that night. Mark was coming at six, since the movie started at six-forty and they had to go back across town to the theater. *I'll be fine by then*, Becca assured herself as she stepped onto the bus.

She threw off her clothes when she got home

and drew her bathrobe around her shivering body. *A little nap will do me a world of good*, she thought, scrounging in the medicine cabinet for something, anything, to take the edge off her queasiness. There was a bottle of some kind of Pepto-Bismol buried behind an assortment of creams and lotions, so she took a teaspoonful.

The house was silent; her father was still at the hospital. She crawled into bed and pulled the pillow over her head to block out the afternoon sunlight. *Come on, Becca, chin up, ready to face the world. This is your life — this is a date, for heaven's sake*. She burrowed deeper under the covers, clenching her teeth against the chill. In a few minutes, she was asleep.

When she woke, it was growing dark outside. She sat up with a heart-stopping lurch. Was she late? The bedside clock read fourthirty.

"Oh, boy!" She held her throbbing head and suppressed the urge to run to the bathroom. She felt awful. Throwing off the covers, she slid her feet out of bed and stood on shaky limbs. It was even difficult to walk normally — everything inside her was churning and roiling. She opened her door and squinted, warding off the bright lights from the living room.

"Hi, Daddy," she murmured, wandering in.

He was straightening some papers on his desk and didn't look up.

"Napping on a Saturday afternoon, eh? Wish I had that luxury. Let me tell you, everyone and his grandmother was checking into Mt. Sinai this afternoon."

"Um." Should she ask him for something to make her feel better? No, he'd never let her go on a date if she was sick. She imagined her father drawing a huge quarantine net around the apartment house. UPSET STOMACH AREA — DANGER, the sign would read in big red letters. It would probably be better not to say anything.

"Well, I better get cracking." Dr. Walters ruffled her hair absently and walked past her into the hallway. "My cousin Ginger is giving a dinner party tonight, so I have to shower and dress. You're very quiet today." He finally turned to look at her white face. "You're all right, aren't you? Feeling okay?" He stretched out a hand to feel her forehead, but she backed off, certain she was running a fever.

"Of course, Daddy. I was just tired, so I lay down, that's all. I have to get moving, too. I'm going to the movies with Mark. You remember, the guy who works at RFB with me?" She turned and half-tripped. She felt dizzy.

"Yes, I think I recall your mentioning him. The boy with the trombone?"

Becca, her back still to her father, gave a

small, bemused groan. "No, Daddy, that's the kid in the school orchestra. Don't you listen when I tell you about people?"

"What? Well, yes, certainly I do. Go get ready now."

At least he has the sense to be embarrassed, she thought as she wandered into the bathroom and turned the shower on. She quickly swallowed a couple of aspirin, hoping they would help her headache, and stepped out of her robe. She was freezing, and she knew their apartment was usually overheated. She made the water as hot as she could take it and then scrubbed her body and hair under the strong current. She toweled herself dry and started for her bedroom to dress, but she caught a glimpse of herself in the mirror on her way out the door, and it stopped her dead in her tracks. Her face was positively green.

"Hi, Becca," she said to her image. "That's fabulous makeup — where'd you get it?" Maybe Mark wouldn't notice. Maybe Mark would catch whatever it was she had and get deathly ill himself. *Don't be silly, he's not going to kiss you good night or anything.*

But then she considered the possibility that he might, and a warm flush took the chill off the room. She'd been kissed before — well, in a manner of speaking. It was last summer, and she'd sort of gotten friendly with this lifeguard at the pool. They didn't have a whole lot in common, but he was very handsome. Just before she was going home one day, Peter hugged her and made a dive for her mouth, but she moved before he got close enough and he kissed the right side of her nose instead. She'd really felt like a jerk.

"Becca, this is no time to daydream," she said aloud, marching to the closet to pick out something wonderful for the evening. But nothing looked great to her right now. There were little silvery dots in front of her eyes. Should she wear a skirt or pants? Blouse or sweater? These decisions, usually pretty easy for her, seemed overwhelming in her present state. Eventually she selected a pair of well-cut plum wool slacks and a lacy white sweater. She'd wear her warm coat and a scarf, even though the weather was pretty mild. That would keep her from shivering. *I ought to have a muffler for my teeth to keep them from chattering*, she thought, fighting down another wave of nausea.

She worked diligently on her makeup, using more blusher than she usually did and outlining her eyes with a dark blue pencil. Camouflage was crucial tonight. The green tinge still showed through, but there was nothing she could do to erase it.

"Dear, I'm on my way," her father called.

She went out into the hallway to say good-bye. He did look nice this evening in his neat gray suit and red tie. He had just had a haircut, so it looked sort of spiky, but he did seem jollier than usual. Maybe there was someone he liked coming to the party, Becca thought suddenly, looking away. She blocked the notion out of her head and tried to picture her father as a teenager, going to pick up his date. She couldn't do it. There was no way that Dr. David Walters had ever been that young.

"I've promised to play chauffeur and pick up some of Ginger's friends, so I better leave now. You'll lock up and everything?"

"Yes, Daddy." He was pulling on his coat. Should she tell him how lousy she felt? "Have a good time."

"You too, dear." He bent over to plant a kiss on her forehead. Couldn't he tell she was burning up? It was that rotten kind of fever where you heard humming in your ears. Thousands of little voices screaming, "Don't go out! Don't go out! Go back to bed!"

"See you later," she murmured as he walked out the door. The elevator clanged shut behind him.

Taking a few deep breaths, Becca plunked herself down on the living room couch and shut her eyes. It was better sitting down, but it still wasn't as good as being tucked under the covers. Her head felt like a huge steel ball attached to her neck, and it was too much trouble to hold it up. She let it fall back against the sofa cushion. There, that was nice. Just the quiet tick of the clock and the distant thrum of the old refrigerator in the kitchen and —

Brrring! The sound of the doorbell jolted her out of her seat. She went racing to answer it, mostly so it wouldn't ring again.

"Oh, hi! You're early!" she panted, leaning on the door frame for support.

"Hi. Yeah, I guess I am, a little."

She led Mark inside, and as their hands accidentally touched, she felt a bit better. She was looking forward to the evening after all. "Do you want anything to drink? A Coke or some juice?"

"No thanks. Why don't we get to the theater, if it's okay with you. I hear the lines for this film are really something."

She noticed that he was wearing brown cords and a tan sweater vest over a brown-and-red plaid shirt. He smelled wonderful, too. Even in her weakened state, she was not oblivious to Mark Shuman's charms. *Judy was right*, she told herself as she went to get her coat. *I wouldn't have missed this for the world.*

"You really want this winter coat?" he asked, helping her into it. "It's not that cold out."

"Yeah, but I've been sort of chilly all day."

She wound the muffler around her neck, flipped the hall lights, and shut the front door behind them. She fiddled with the lock, her fingers refusing to put the key in the correct place. She was still shivering, even dressed to the gills as she was.

"I'll do it," Mark said, taking the key ring from her. As he did so, their hands touched again, and this time, he looked at her curiously. "You really are cold. Are you feeling okay?"

"Yeah, sure," she affirmed with a brightness she didn't feel at all. *This is dumb. Just tell him — he'll understand.* But she didn't want to spoil anything, so she kept her mouth shut.

She didn't do much talking on the bus ride to the movie theater, but let Mark talk about this particular filmmaker and his other work. It was really interesting, but she kept having to swallow and take deep breaths, and she was sure he must think he was boring her. Her glazed eyes felt so hot, they were like fried eggs on a griddle.

They did have to wait on line after they got their tickets, and standing in one place became unbearable for Becca. Sometimes she thought she was going to fall down; other times she felt like she'd never be able to lift her feet when the line started moving. *If only*

I could lean my head on his shoulder, she mused, trying to keep up her brave front. *If only I could tell him the truth!* But her inner sense of what was right and appropriate to the situation wouldn't let her.

Finally, they were allowed to inch forward, and Becca let the crowd and Mark's guiding arm propel her toward the theater door. The seat in the darkened movie house loomed in her mind like an oasis, lush with green trees and cooling breezes and the heavenly scent of fresh water. She would sink back into it and close her eyes and —

"Becca! Are you sure you're not sick or something? You look like you're about to pass out." Mark's voice came to her through a fog of discomfort, filled with kindness and concern.

"Well, I . . ." *Say it, dummy! Tell him!* "I sort of had a stomachache this morning. I was sure it would go away by now."

"You want to go home?"

"Oh, no!" They were now at the head of the line, and Mark hesitated before handing their tickets to the man at the door.

"Hurry up, will you, buddy?" said a burly, redheaded man behind them.

"Let's go in, Mark." Becca nodded. "I'm really not that bad."

"Well, just tell me if you are. Promise?"

She was too weak to do anything but nod her head.

They took their seats amid the hubbub and jostling of the crowd. Becca was so thankful to set her five-hundred-pound head down on the seat back that she didn't even bother to take off her coat. In a few minutes, the lights dimmed and the curtains parted in front of the large screen.

"Oh, great, a trailer. I really live for the trailers. Usually they're better than the feature," Mark whispered.

"I know what you mean," Becca smiled, allowing her weight to shift toward him. Her body felt so heavy and placid, like she'd been weighted down with an anchor and allowed to float to the bottom of the sea. Aside from her stomach cramps, the feeling was not at all unpleasant. And what made it much nicer was the presence of Mark at her side. *He really is pretty terrific*, she thought before she melted away into a feverish trance. The picture on the screen flickered before her eyes. She heard the actors' voices through a dim veil.

She didn't know how long she'd been that way, half-unconscious, half-attempting to be a perfectly normal girl on a date, when she was hit with an uncontrollable need to throw up. She couldn't speak; she simply dove across Mark and the three people closest to the aisle and dashed toward the exit sign, her pocket-book flopping from one hand, the other pressed over her mouth. Thank goodness she'd been in this theater before and vaguely remembered where the ladies' room was. She made it to the stall just in time and flung the toilet seat up as she knelt before it. The sickness didn't want to leave her, but eventually, after a few half-hearted gags, she was able to bring something up.

She stayed there quietly for a few minutes and then, careful not to jar anything, keeping her head level, she slowly stood up and walked out of the stall. She ran the water in the sink as cold as she could get it and, with barely a thought to messing up her makeup, she splashed great handfuls in her face and on the back of her neck. Then she let her head sink down on the cool porcelain. She listened to the gentle gurgle of the water beside her face and she slowly stood up, breathing easily once more. She felt better.

Patting her face and hands dry with the rough paper towel, she wandered back out into the hallway. Mark was leaning against the opposite wall under a poster of coming attractions. He came to her immediately and took her hands in his.

"Hey, we're taking you home right now. No argument."

"Mark, really, I want to stay. I, uh, took care of everything." She jerked her thumb toward the bathroom. "I'm all better now."

He shook his head and made a face that reminded her of her father when he listened to one of her stories with extreme skepticism. "I guess you're a martyr or something. But just . . . would you let me know when you've had enough?"

"Sure." She tugged on his hand and they went through the door together, back into the comforting dark. The sound of a noisy cattle stampede, somewhere in New Zealand, filled the theater.

"I wouldn't mind missing the end of this, you know," he said softly as they found their seats again. "It's not as good as his last flick."

"Well, I like it," she declared staunchly.

"Shhh!" Several people around them gave them annoyed looks as they settled down. This time, Mark held her hand, and that made her feel one hundred percent better. She ignored the rumbles and groans coming from the vicinity of her stomach and concentrated hard, determined to enjoy what remained of the movie.

"I don't know, I think he had his characters going at cross-purposes," Mark was saying. "You look green again." He had barely touched his hamburger and 7-Up when he saw how difficult it was for Becca to even taste the tea and toast she had ordered at the coffee shop near the theater. This time, he didn't listen when she assured him she was okay and whisked her outside and hailed a cab. It had just started to drizzle, and the cool drops felt funny on her hot face. She almost wanted to suggest that they walk home, but she decided she was probably feverish, and walking in that condition might bring on pneumonia. The nausea was worse than ever.

She let him guide her into her apartment house and handed him the keys in the elevator. All she could think about was going to sleep and staying that way for a couple of days.

He opened the door and flipped the hall light switch. "How about trying some tea again? I'll make you a cup — where's the kitchen?"

"In there." She pointed rather reluctantly. "I don't really feel like any, though."

"Well, I do. I'm hungry. Come on, I'm a fantastic tea-brewer." They walked from the soft carpeting of the dining room to the kitchen linoleum, and the brittle sound of their heels on the floor made Becca wince. She'd just about had it with acting. It seemed impossible to play hostess, feeling the way she did.

Mark rummaged around in the places she pointed to and set out tea and bags and the sugar bowl, after putting the kettle on to boil.

"My sister uses this stuff to steam her face," he chuckled. "She is the vainest thing I've ever seen. Didn't used to be so bad before she went to college, but you know, *Bryn Mawr!*" He stressed the name like it was the height of ridiculousness. "Every time she comes home for a vacation or a weekend, she's more stuck-up. So one morning I find her with towels all over her head and she's inhaling this pot of tea over the sink. I thought she was going nuts, but she said it was a facial and I should mind my own business."

Becca didn't hear the end of the sentence. She was on her feet and running toward the bathroom, holding herself around the middle to keep everything together. When she reached the bathroom, there was no time to do anything but fling herself headlong over the toilet bowl, letting the illness pour out of her. Great heaves took over, making her helpless. Even when she thought there could be no more and she was too exhausted to take another breath, it was not over. Again and again she retched. Her mind went blank — all that was left was a humming sound, the pulse of her own heart, raggedly beating.

She felt a hand on her arm. She made herself look up. "Oh, God, go away!" To her enormous chagrin, she realized that Mark was right beside her, sitting on the edge of the tub, watching. How long had he been there? Automatically, she reached over and flushed the toilet, slamming the lid down.

"Here, let me." He had a damp washcloth in his hand, and he set it as close to her forehead as she would let him. She felt her stomach turning again and prayed she would not have to be sick again with him still sitting there.

"Please get out, please," she begged, grabbing the washcloth to dab at her mouth. "I don't want you here." She was crying now.

"Becca, stop fighting me. Look, you're a mess. I'm going to help, whether you like it or not." He reached across with his other hand to smooth a few bedraggled strands of hair out of her face.

"I want my father," she sobbed, sitting back on her heels and biting down on the washcloth so that her words were obscured. "He's a doctor; he can take care of me. Please go get him." Somewhere, deep inside, she wondered whether she was only saying this to get Mark out of the bathroom. She was so embarrassed.

"Becca, he isn't here. He hasn't come home yet. For heaven's sake, let me —"

"No!" she cut him off. "Get out of here! I'm not allowed to be alone with a guy in the apartment," she lied. Her father had never mentioned such a rule, but it sounded good and plausible the minute she said it. It was the perfect way to get rid of Mark — probably forever.

Where *was* her father? He was supposed to be here when she was sick, instead of gallivanting around town, squiring ladies he wasn't married to. Maybe he'd stay out all night! If he did that, she'd never speak to him again. How could he have let her go on a date when she was so sick! She hated him — her mother was right to leave him. The last thing she wanted was to have Mark Shuman see her like this. It was all her father's fault.

Mark shrugged and gazed at Becca intently, the deep brown color of his eyes becoming warmer and softer even as she looked at him. "I'm sorry," he said in a small voice. "I'll shut the door on my way out."

She waited until she heard the lock click before she dared to stand up. Her legs were wobbly and it took all her strength to walk over to the sink. Again she ran the cold water, rinsing her mouth before taking a few sips. She felt so tired, so totally done in. The idea of staying in bed forever flitted through her mind. *That'd serve him right*, she thought smugly, looking past the bedraggled face with smeared eye makeup that peered at her from the mirror.

She let her clothes fall where they would, making a pile around her feet. She didn't even bother to put on her nightgown, but huddled back into her bathrobe because it was warmer. Her teeth were really chattering now. She pulled the blankets up and tucked her feet into the pockets made by her bent knees. Why couldn't she just let sleep claim her, take her away to that magic land where things were hazy and rose-colored? Oddly enough, she wasn't tired. She was lonely.

She knew the number by heart now, so she turned on the bedside lamp and picked up the phone receiver. First the area code, then the number. It would only be a little after nine in Michigan now. The phone rang three times, then someone answered.

"Hello, Mom? It's me."

"Honey! Hold on a sec. I've got something on the stove. Be right back."

Becca snuggled under the covers again and put the receiver on the pillow so she could lie next to it. The sound of her mother's voice was so clear and close, it was like she was in the next room. If only she could come walking through the bedroom door now, carrying a glass of Coke with two aspirins crushed into it. Before Becca was able to swallow pills, her parents used to try to deceive her.

"It tastes funny," Becca would say, wrinkling her nose.

"That's just because your taste buds are

sick," her mother would answer. Becca never believed her, but she drank the stuff, anyway.

"Sweetheart! I'm sorry — I was just fixing a late dinner for myself. How's everything? I've been at the library all night. It's such a treat to hear a human voice!"

"Oh, Mom," Becca wailed. She hated to sound like a whiny kid, but she felt so miserable, and she'd never needed her mother more than at this very instant. She blurted out the whole awful tale of her date as Rachel listened patiently on the other end of the line.

"That stinks," was her mother's assessment when at last Becca finished in a burst of tears. "But he sounds like a nice boy. You probably haven't seen the last of him."

"Well, I have to see him every day," Becca sobbed, "because we work together. It'll be so horrible."

"No, listen," Rachel said soothingly. "One day you'll be standing in a quiet corner in the stacks and he'll come up behind you and whisper sweet nothings in your ear. It'll be dreamy!"

"Oh, Mom," Becca sniffed, laughing in spite of herself. "You're an incurable romantic."

"Uh-huh. I sure am."

"It'll be so good to see you. I can't wait till Christmas." Becca gripped the phone tightly.

"Oh, honey, I forgot. I meant to tell you. I'm afraid I . . . Christmas is out. My exam schedule is a killer — four in a row starting the day after vacation ends. I'd be studying the whole time — it would be awful for you."

"I'll come, anyway. Please, can I? I'll be quiet when you're working, and I'll make all the meals. I've . . . we've become pretty good cooks, me and Daddy."

"How *is* your father?" her mother asked in a different, more serious voice.

"He's okay. Fine, actually. Please say I can come." She was desperate to have something to look forward to. If her mother had agreed, she would have packed a bag and gone to the airport that very night, even if she lost her stomach along the way.

"Hey, I'd be too tempted to have fun with you around, darling. It just can't be. But spring break, that's a different story. We'll have a marvelous time. None of these dratted avalanches and ice storms. We'll go shopping, you'll meet my new friends — oh, Becca." Her voice dropped half an octave, and she sighed deeply. "I wish I could see you. It's really weird without you, you know that?"

Becca's throat constricted and she wanted to be with her mother more than ever. "I miss you, too, Mom. What's it like for you, going back to school?" She wanted to ask what it was like being without a husband and kid after being so used to them for years and years, but she couldn't get the words out. Wasn't it funny for her mother to be surrounded by college kids? Although she recalled her mother had always preferred to consider herself a kid rather than a grown-up.

"It's neat, really!" Rachel said a little too enthusiastically. "The place, the people — they're all wonderful. I hope you apply to Michigan when it comes time for your college applications. That's soon, isn't it? We could set up housekeeping and be two college girls together. What do you say?"

Becca knew her mother was trying to cheer her up, but it really wasn't working. She just wanted plain old TLC tonight — nothing complicated like thoughts of the future. "Maybe. I was thinking of applying closer to home, though," she muttered, turning over on her stomach to press it into the mattress. She felt another wave of sickness and began coughing to hold back the nausea.

"Honey, you really sound awful! When your father gets home, you get him to give you something."

"Uh," Becca grunted.

"Promise now. Hey, the boy sounds pretty super to me. A definitely good catch — congratulations."

"I think I hear Daddy now," Becca said quickly, swallowing hard. "Got to say good night, okay?"

The truth was, she didn't want to think about Mark, or about what she'd done to spoil the evening — and maybe a lot more — by her stupidness. It wasn't something she could explain, even to her mother.

"Okay, darling, talk to you soon. Bye-bye." Her mother hung up and Becca hugged the receiver to her chest for a moment. Her mother was miles away, farther than a plane could ever take her. It just didn't feel the same, trying to get through.

She dropped the receiver onto its cradle and huddled back into the warm embrace of the blankets. "I want my father," she murmured softly. Then she closed her eyes and sleep took over.

Six

Becca was only able to drag herself out of bed after four long days of flu. Her father had been livid, of course, and demanded to know, even as he took her temperature and gave her something to quell the nausea, why she had done such a stupid thing and not told him.

Her sick days were a timeless kaleidoscope of sleep and dozing beside the radio and making frequent trips to the bathroom. Every so often, when she opened her eyes, she would see her father sitting across the room at her desk chair, immersed in a medical journal or doing his bills. He never wasted time, unlike Becca.

At last, on the fourth day, feeling weak but finally alert, Becca appeared at the breakfast table in her robe. She'd wanted to shower and dress first, but she didn't want to miss her father in case he left early for the office.

"What are you doing out of bed?" he asked sternly, looking over his glasses at her.

"I'm better," she shrugged, taking a seat. "Can I have some coffee?"

"Tea," he responded, getting up to put the kettle back on. "Did you take your temperature?"

"It's normal," she sighed, reaching for a piece of toast. At last she was hungry, and it felt good.

"That boy called last night." Her father placed the teapot on a trivet and turned to stare at her, a butterfly collector regarding a prized specimen. "He wanted to know how you were."

"Mark called?" She couldn't believe it. "What did he say? What did you tell him?"

"I simply explained the situation. Who is this boy, Becca? Have I ever met him?"

If you'd been home like you were supposed to be, you would have. "No, Daddy, he's the one from my job, remember? He's in my class at Halsted, too, but I really never knew him before this year."

"Was he aware that you were ill when you went out?"

What is this, the third degree? Why couldn't her father leave her alone? Couldn't he see she was weak and tired? That supermarket shopping spree and dinner date must have been a lapse, and now he regretted ever acting like a human being. *How did Mom ever take him for sixteen whole years?*

"I told him I was fine and he believed me — what was he supposed to do? He really tried to get me home early, but it was my fault — I wanted to stay out."

How great that Mark called. He's terrific, no question about it. Why was I so mean to him?

"Well, if your relationship continues, I think it would be appropriate for me to get acquainted with him."

"Sure. Great. Listen, Daddy, you're going to be late."

He glanced at his watch, then gave her that nervous, worried look again. "You'll stay in bed one more day. Continue the medication, and I want you to drink lots of liquids." He slipped his jacket over his starchy white shirt and buttoned it. "I'll be back from the clinic by five."

"Okay. I'll need a note for school tomorrow."

"If you're well," he said cautiously, picking

up his coat and his black bag in the hall. "I'll make that determination in the morning." He looked at her once more, then closed the door behind him.

"Yes, gentlemen, we shall determine whether conditions are appropriate for rocket launch in the morning," Becca said to the dining room table. "These and other matters of state will be reported to the American public only after we are certain there are no security leaks." She sighed, picked up her cup of tea, and went back to bed.

She did go to school on Thursday, and every free minute was taken up with borrowing notes from classes she'd missed. There was an English composition due on Monday and a history quiz the following Thursday. She'd kept up with her French assignments, at least, but she was completely lost in trigonometry. She'd have to bury herself in her books over the weekend — maybe Judy could come over and help her catch up.

She was so busy during the day, she hardly had time to look around for Mark. Naturally, he was on her mind, and she couldn't decide whether she was more anxious about seeing him or about not seeing him. Why had she been so awful to him? If he never spoke to her again, she'd certainly deserve it.

"I was sick, I was out of my mind, Mark —

I didn't know what I was saying." You sound just like your mother. Don't make fantastic excuses, just apologize, clearly and simply.

By the time she got to work that afternoon, she knew exactly what to say. But when she saw Mark talking with Mr. Gormley, her bravado dissolved and she went and hid in the stacks. She worked late and was the last one out. The cleaning lady found her sorting tapes in a corner and gave a little surprised shriek. Becca apologized to *her* and left quickly.

On Friday night, she began wondering why she didn't return Mark's phone call. She buckled down and wrestled with her homework instead.

Saturday, she had her violin lesson. It seemed pointless going this week, since she hadn't practiced more than a couple of hours. But it was another excuse to get out of the house, and she always enjoyed talking with Ms. Claymore. Some days, her teacher would pick up her instrument to show Becca a particularly difficult fingering and would get so caught up in playing, the hour would just fly by. Ms. Claymore was too good to be teaching reluctant teenagers who'd rather be shopping or hanging out with friends. Becca often came close to telling her so, but she never did, fearing it might hurt her teacher's feelings.

She left as soon as her lesson was over,

promising to work doubly hard for the next week. Should she drop in on Judy? She was in the neighborhood, and the Sterns never minded company. But if they got to talking, Judy would grill her about Mark and would undoubtedly rake her over the coals about her behavior. Judy already had five elaborate schemes as to how to patch things up and get Mark to ask Becca out again. Becca had told her point-blank that she didn't operate that way, but Judy was hard to convince.

No, she decided, wandering down Broadway. She didn't really want company today. She'd do a little window-shopping and cut over to Fifth at the park. Then she'd eventually get to the Museum of Modern Art. A nice lunch in the cafeteria and a leisurely tour of the Picassos.

She stopped on Columbus Avenue in a hosiery store to buy a pair of pantyhose. She'd just made her selection and was about to hand the package to the saleswoman, when she spotted a familiar head. Nobody else had frizzy red hair that wild!

"Joanie, hi."

The other girl whirled around as though she'd been smacked. She was the same crimson color she'd been that day in the recordings library when Mark introduced them.

"Sorry, I didn't mean to startle you," Becca

said softly, noticing that Joanie's hands, holding a couple of pairs of pantyhose, were visibly shaking. *What is it with her?* Becca mused. *It's almost like she expects people to hit her instead of say hello.*

"It's okay . . . okay," Joanie murmured, collecting herself. She put the two packages of hose back in the pile.

"Didn't you find what you wanted?" Becca asked, determined to draw the girl out.

"These are . . . they're sort of dark, don't you think?" Joanie whispered.

"Oh, I don't know. Well, yes, I see your point. Something more buff-colored would probably be better for every day." Somehow, she gathered what the problem was. "Oh, m'am," she said to the salesperson, a peroxided blond wearing makeup about two inches thick. "Do you have these in a lighter color?"

The woman stared at them both, then cracked her gum with a resounding pop. "Yeah, I guess. What size?"

"A," Becca answered for Joanie, sensing that she couldn't.

"Just a sec." The woman disappeared in the back and Joanie's face lit up in an almost painful show of gratitude. "How did you . . ." she began, but Becca cut in, "I'm a real loudmouth, I guess. I didn't mean to barge in."

"No, it's fine." The two girls stared at each

other, and in that quick moment, they understood each other. The salesperson returned
with several bundles of hose bound together
with rubber bands, and they didn't even notice
when she held them out.

"Hey." She cleared her throat and moved
her gum to the other side of her mouth. "You
want these?"

"Sure." Becca snatched at them and the
saleswoman looked at them both as though
they were bonkers. Then she shrugged and
her expression changed as if to say, "What the
hell, it's New York, what do you expect?"

Becca and Joanie paid for two pairs apiece
and walked out of the store together. "I'm
going to the Modern," Becca offered. "Want
to come?"

"Oh, I can't really, I have to get home."
Joanie turned and without a word of good-
bye, she left Becca standing there.

What a flake! she thought, shaking her head
and continuing down the avenue. *You'd think
her parents beat her, or something.* Then she
bit her lip, realizing that in this day and age
that was not such a farfetched notion. Joanie's
terrible shyness had to come from somewhere.
Maybe her folks didn't beat her physically,
but she sure was a mess emotionally.

Becca hugged her violin case to her chest
and kept walking. *At least I have a father who*

loves me, she thought. *He may be a pain at times, he may be critical and insensitive and overprotective, but he's a pretty good egg. And I seem to have turned out all right. Thank goodness I can ask a salesperson for a pair of pantyhose. When I can't do that anymore, I'll know it's time for the bin!*

The only thing she seemed incapable of doing was to face Mark and talk things out. She managed to procrastinate and avoid him for two entire weeks. It was a miraculous maneuver of always being in the wrong place at the wrong time. If she saw Mark coming, she'd either glom onto Joanie or disappear into an office or walk away. The more she stayed away from him, the more it became clear that she had to continue what she'd started. She hated herself, but she couldn't stop the feelings of shame and chagrin. She wished she could disappear — then she wouldn't have to deal with the problem at all.

But at last her strategy failed, and she was enormously relieved when it did. It was hard, running away all the time.

One evening at work it came to a head. She was in the middle of taping a rather dull botany text, when there was a loud pop and the recorder stopped functioning. Becca fiddled with it for several minutes before acknowledging defeat.

"I'm really sorry," she told the scientist, pushing her long hair away from her face before stepping outside the studio. "I have to get someone to fix it."

Mark was just down the hall, editing a tape. She looked through the small glass window and the sight of him, his hair flopping over his forehead, his sleeves rolled up, his brow furrowed in concentration, made her glad that she was interrupting him.

"Ah, excuse me, I —"

He popped out of his seat, hitting his hip against the desk. "Ow! Hi, what's up?" He was grinning at her, so things couldn't be all bad, could they?

"I'm, uh, my machine isn't going. I've tried everything, but I guess you better look at it."

"Be right with you." He rolled his tape back to the beginning and put a white plastic marker at the point where he'd stopped. She watched his hands accomplish everything swiftly and efficiently. They were small hands, not particularly hairy, but they were very agile and muscular. She liked the look of them.

"Okay." He put the cover back on the machine and stuck the tape he'd been working on at the edge of the nearest shelf. He followed her down the corridor in silence and she wondered, *What's he thinking? Is he going to talk to me after this is over?* She didn't dare look at him for fear of blushing if he caught her at it.

"Dr. Van Dusen, we may have to reschedule some of this taping. I'm really sorry," she said hurriedly as Mark began to examine the machine. "All the other rooms are occupied right now. Could you come down to Mrs. Samuels's office with me and make another appointment?"

The man looked disgruntled, but didn't put up a fuss. He gathered up his books and coat with a sigh and a half-muttered comment about having more important things to do.

"Becca, there's no chance I can fix this tonight. One of these gizmos is completely worn out." Mark shrugged, pushing his hair back out of his eyes.

How come his mother doesn't tell him to get a haircut? Becca wondered as she led Dr. Van Dusen back down the corridor. *My father always lets me know when I'm too shaggy. But he does look kind of cute this way.*

She was excessively polite and apologetic to the scientist, gave him another date, and took the papers Mrs. Samuels gave her to file. Mark's office was on her way to the filing cabinets, and he practically shouted at her when she came into view.

"Becca! Come here a minute, will you?"

She bit her lip and walked through the side entrance of his cubicle. She was breathing hard.

"I think we have something to talk about," he said in a much lower voice. "What about a Coke? It's almost closing time."

She wanted to say no because she liked him so much and she knew he was mad at her for her behavior over the past two weeks. She wanted to say yes because everything about him was so kind and sympathetic and easy to adjust to. How was it possible to feel so many different things at one time? So what she finally said was:

"I'll have to call my father and ask. He expects me home right after work, see?"

"Sure, well, go ahead. Then let me know. I'll be waiting down by reception."

She padded down the corridor, back to her cubicle. Of course, she could always say she'd called and couldn't get permission. That would settle the whole thing forever. Mark would assume she didn't want to go out with him and probably not try again.

How stupid! You are really dumb! You want to go out with him, right? Well then, you can't avoid the explanation. So he'll yell at you for acting like a ninny — it won't be the end of the world, you know. People do have arguments and make up, unlike your parents.

Then it hit her like a thunderbolt. That was why she didn't want to confront Mark! She picked up the phone and dialed home.

"Hi, Daddy. It's me. Have a nice day?"

"It was fine, dear. Where are you?

"Still at work. Listen, you know that guy I went to the movies with the night I got so sick? He just asked me to have a Coke with him before dinner. Is that okay? I'll be about half an hour late."

"You mean right now? He's asked you out on such short notice?"

Becca rolled her eyes to the ceiling in exasperation. "Hey, Daddy, I don't need a formal invitation. Absolutely nobody sends back those little engraved RSVP's just for a can of Coke these days."

There was a sharp intake of breath on the other end of the line. "Don't get smart with me, young lady. I still make the decisions about when you're expected home."

"I know." Becca immediately regretted her answer. It was so unlike her — what had gotten into her, to say something like that to her father?

"About how long would you be?" he asked softly.

"Only half an hour, I promise." Her whole attitude had changed during the brief conversation. Now she *wanted* to go out with Mark — she *had* to. If she didn't get everything straight with him this evening, she never would.

"Well, I'll give my permission tonight on the express understanding that this doesn't become a habit. And I'd like to meet this fellow in the very near future if you intend keeping company with him. Am I making myself quite clear, Becca?"

"Oh, yes, Daddy. And thank you. I'll be home soon."

"See that you are. I'll keep your lamb chops warm in the oven. A new experiment of mine — I hope you like them."

"Of course I will. 'Bye, Daddy."

She replaced the receiver gently, thinking about her father in the kitchen. He sounded like a lost child, as if he'd wanted her home not because he was the rule-maker but because he actually needed her. Was it possible, she wondered as she slowly put on her coat and gathered up her things? Her father wanted to be with her — it wasn't just that he had to because he was her father.

Lost in thought, she trailed down the corridor to the front desk. Mark was hunkered down on his heels, flipping through a copy of *Playboy*.

"Well, what's the verdict?" he asked with an amused grin as she came into view.

"I can go," she nodded, "if it's only half an hour."

"Great!" He was evidently very happy about

this. He picked up his magazine, stuffed it into his book bag, and wrapped his scarf around his neck. "Shall we?" He made a gallant bow. Although she still felt awkward, his attitude made it a bit easier.

"What shape is that machine in?" she asked quickly as they hurried into the cool November evening. Maybe a little chitchat first would pave the way toward their serious discussion.

"Too tough for me," he shrugged, readily admitting he was licked. "All I know is it's in the reel-to-reel mechanism. Something's burned out, I guess. I left a note for Johnny to look at it first thing in the morning. How about Phoebe's?" He pointed at the hamburger place on the corner of Sixty-third Street.

"Fine. I can't stay long."

"You already said that. I'll talk fast."

Becca smiled nervously as he opened the door for her. It was warm inside, and the smells of perked coffee, cigarette smoke, and cooking hamburgers assailed her along with the murmurs of many different conversations. There was a table for two in the corner and they settled themselves at it. A waitress brought them menus.

"Just a Coke, please," Becca told her.

"I'll live dangerously," Mark said. "Coke and a corn muffin."

As the woman walked away, scribbling on

her pad, Mark leaned across the table and whispered conspiratorially, "My mother never cooks enough. I usually grab a bite either before or after dinner."

"Why don't you tell her you're hungry?" Becca asked, puzzled, unfolding her napkin on her lap.

"Naw. Don't want to hurt her feelings. See, she's really into Japanese cooking where everything looks great but there's never enough on one plate to feed a pigmy. She's always trying to put my father on a diet, but he cheats."

"Hmm. What's your father do?"

"He's an accountant. But not like you'd imagine."

"What do you mean?"

The waitress set their orders in front of them and ripped a check from her pad.

"Oh, he's not a three-pack-a-day worrier who brings his calculator to the breakfast table. You know, he has interests other than money. Actually, his passion is astronomy. He's up on the roof of our apartment house every clear night, no matter what the temperature, glued to his telescope."

"That's neat," said Becca, wishing her father had a hobby. *I'm his hobby*, she thought appraisingly. *No, more like his ball and chain*.

"Yeah, he's a good guy," Mark nodded. "So yours is a doctor, huh?" He took a long slurp of his Coke. "So, what are you guys doing for Thanksgiving?" he asked.

"Oh, um, nothing special," Becca shrugged.

"Just ordinary relatives, right?"

"Well, actually," she began slowly, "we're going out to a French restaurant."

Mark stared at her incredulously, then burst out laughing.

"What's so funny?" She grimaced, feeling annoyed and as if she wanted to get up and leave him sitting right there, laughing.

"A French restaurant? You're kidding!"

"No, I mean it," she said staunchly. "We were going to go to my uncle's up in Westchester, but we changed that to Christmas — it turned out they were going to his in-laws' home for Thanksgiving. So my father suggested a fancy meal out."

"That's wild. I never heard of anything like that," Mark said.

Secretly, Becca felt it was a rotten idea, but she didn't want to criticize her father. All she could think of as an explanation was, "Well, we have a really small family, see?"

"Right. Well, it should be interesting, I'll say that. Sometimes I want to crawl into a cave and hibernate from the end of November till after the New Year. It can be more family than you ever knew about — or wanted to know about." He leaned back and stared at her appraisingly. "Becca, can I ask you something?"

Uh-oh. Here it comes. She wished he didn't change subjects so quickly — he gave her no time to prepare answers. "Sure. What is it?"

"Why are you so scared of me?"

"Huh? It's . . . I'm not!" she responded hotly.

"First we go on this date, and you're about to die but you don't tell anybody. Then, when I make a valiant attempt to resuscitate the corpse, you throw me out of your house. Then I make a nice, polite phone call to your not-so-polite father and it doesn't get returned. Then" — he poked his straw at her — "you hide every time you see me for two weeks."

"It wasn't two weeks," she murmured, staring into her Coke.

"Ten days, whatever. All I can make of all this is that you're scared. Either that, or your father is the proverbial dragon who keeps his beautiful daughter all locked up from nasty young boys." He leaned across the table, offering her a bite of his corn muffin.

"No, thanks." She waved it away but he didn't move. He obviously wouldn't budge until she gave him an answer.

"It's not because of my father, honest. I mean, he's strict, but that whole episode was my fault entirely. Once I'd started acting crazy, I couldn't stop," she confessed.

"Well, I'm glad to hear *you* say it," he chuckled, settling back in his seat at last. "I didn't want to be rude."

"No, it's true. I just got really tied up in knots about doing the right thing at the right time, you know?"

"Sure." He bit into his muffin with relish. "Well, I was really worried about you. That's why I called. And since then, I've been doing everything I could think of to break the ice. You sure make it hard, lady."

"How do you mean my father wasn't polite?" She frowned.

"He didn't seem happy about delivering the message is all I can say." Mark shrugged. "I mean, I got the Big Freeze over the phone."

"Oh, well." Becca gulped. "Some people aren't good on the telephone. You ought to meet him in person."

"Yeah? When?"

"I . . . well, I just meant . . ." She looked into his determined gaze. It was almost a challenge, as if he was telling her he could accomplish any trial she put in his path. If she wanted him to fight the dragon for her, he would. "Say" — she gazed right back at him — "how about dinner right after Thanksgiving? My father and I are becoming *the* meat loaf specialists of New York. And I promise you'll get enough to eat."

"Don't you have to check this with your mother first?"

Becca swallowed, then shook her head. He didn't know! Well, of course not, why should he? "My mother's in Michigan," she began carefully.

"Oh? Visiting relatives or something?"

"No, she's at school, getting her master's. She's . . . well, my parents are separated, getting divorced."

"Huh? Really? And you're living with your father? Did you make that choice?"

He didn't seem at all judgmental or overly solicitous like Judy and her family. He just seemed curious.

"There sort of wasn't a choice. I mean, I couldn't leave Halsted right before senior year."

"Yeah, and Michigan's pretty cold, I hear. So your father's cooking, too. That's great. Good for him." Mark put down the money for their check as he glanced at his watch. "Well, in case he's made you a soufflé, you better not be late." He took one last sip of his Coke before pushing back his chair.

"You'll come, then? The week after next — after Thanksgiving?" Becca asked.

"It's a date." Together they walked outside and started toward the subway.

"Anything in particular you don't eat?"

"Fruit." He nodded emphatically. "I hate all kinds of fruit."

"You do? That's weird!" Becca giggled.

"I know. Well, what can I say? You'll have to take me, warts and all. You and your father."

"We'll look forward to it," she murmured as they started down the steps to the IRT.

Seven

Thanksgiving was worse than Becca could ever have imagined. She and her father were the only Americans in the whole restaurant, and even the waiters seemed amused to see them. Becca wanted turkey and all the trimmings, but what she got was duck *à l'orange*. Her father was jolly and cheery and unusually talkative, but it was hard to get into the holiday mood when surrounded by posters of Normandy with Edith Piaf songs coming from the speakers.

They did discuss Mark, though, and to

Becca's surprise, her father was delighted with the idea of having a dinner guest. "We haven't entertained at all, now that I think of it," he declared. "This'll give me a chance to perfect my chili. Or would you prefer my chicken *à la moutarde*?" He smoothed his small, rusty-colored mustache in imitation of the French maître d' who had seated them so ceremoniously, and Becca started giggling. Her father could really astound her sometimes.

"I guess chili," she grinned, glad that he was willing to keep things casual for Mark. She had expected him to act like the Prince of Wales was coming to dinner, but maybe the stuffiness of the French restaurant had shown him the light. Now all she had to worry about was that he and Mark would get along.

Mark had asked her to go to another movie with him that Sunday — "as my reward for putting up with all those relatives," as he put it — and it was another surprise to Becca how glad she was to see him after only a three-day hiatus.

They went to a Humphrey Bogart double bill, and Becca forgot everything as she watched the two stories unfold before them on the screen. Things had been so different then between people, was what occurred to her when they walked out of the theater several hours later. People stuck by each other —

they had a sense of commitment. Not like today. She was sobbing and couldn't stop, and Mark reached up to brush the wet drops from her face as other couples pushed past them, hurrying to hail cabs or rush into nearby restaurants. It was cold.

"You know, it's only a movie," he assured her.

"I know, but it means something, don't you see? People are . . . oh, sometimes they're so messed up." She couldn't explain her reaction. It was like each piece of film was stuck in a loop running over and over inside her head.

"Becca, if they're messed up, it's their problem, not yours. I think you take things too personally."

"That's right." She snuffled back her tears, and then laughed. "I think the great big design of things was molded right on me. Pretty selfish, huh?"

"Not selfish, just silly." He shrugged. "You gotta learn to have fun. And I'll be damned if I'm gonna stop trying to make you enjoy yourself!"

"Please, please — keep up the effort." Becca smiled weakly. "Sorry I got so emotional." She hastily wiped her face.

"I like you like that — shows you're not dead." When she looked aghast, he looped an arm through hers and pulled her forward.

"Look, lots of people are. Just tell me one thing. When I come for dinner at your house, do I have to wear a suit and tie?"

"Oh, no, certainly not." She grimaced and shook her head. He was changing the subject again, to throw her off guard. "*He* will, of course, but that doesn't mean you have to. He virtually sleeps with his tie on, so don't worry about it."

"But I want to make an impression."

Mark was grinning, and Becca suddenly saw he was teasing her, giving her back a taste of her own attitude about taking everything too personally.

"You've already made an impression on *me*. He doesn't count."

"Oh, I think he counts a lot in your book."

Mark knew her so well; it was impossible to keep secrets from him anymore. *And why should I?* she thought. They walked on, even though it had started to rain. Becca felt better already.

The following Friday, she and her father got everything ready and made the chili, which, as her father always insisted, had to relax a day in the refrigerator to develop its true flavor. Mrs. Parkhurst had cleaned the apartment within an inch of its life, so there wasn't much else to do other than the salad and dessert, which Becca offered to bring home after her violin lesson the following morning. Flowers, too, she decided, although she didn't tell her father. She didn't want to go overboard on how important this dinner was to her.

Promptly at noon the next day, she opened the door to their apartment, laden with packages, her cheeks rosy from the cold.

"I'm back," she began to call out, but suddenly she saw her father standing at the end of the hallway. His back was to her, but she knew that stance. That defeated, stooped man he sometimes turned into.

"Daddy?" she asked hesitantly, closing the door softly. She walked over to him, but he didn't move. He was still wearing his coat and holding up a sheaf of legal-sized papers, joined at the top with a blue band. The rest of the morning's mail was lying in a pile at his feet where he had dropped, or perhaps thrown it. Becca couldn't tell if he was sad or angry or something else.

"What is it? What's the matter?" She came to him and touched his arm, but he didn't seem to notice. He was lost in some world of his own. She read over his shoulder: *Divorce Proceedings: Rachel Walters/David B. Walters.*

"It's over," he said quietly. "I simply didn't think it would happen so quickly. How long has she been gone? Twelve weeks, is it?"

The divorce was final, then. Her parents

were legally and formally extricated from one another's lives, and she was the only remaining proof of their union. She was swept by a gigantic range of emotion, from terror to desolation to relief. There was no hope anymore that her parents would ever be getting back together. That sheaf of paper was testimony to how badly her mother wanted to call it quits. Well, Rachel had a new life now, one that didn't include Becca or her father. And all they had was each other, and their sorrow.

"I don't know why it seems so strange to me," her father muttered, sitting heavily on the chair beside the telephone. "I just never believed it would actually happen. It happens to other people."

Becca looked at him, and for the first time in her life, she saw him as a man, just a plain, small man, not her larger-than-life father. She felt so tender toward him, as though she could reach out and embrace him like a little baby and cause all the pain to go away. But something held her back — was it embarrassment? *He needs you now — you have to be good to him,* ran through her mind over and over. She bent down and picked up the rest of the mail, then stood before him, holding it.

"Why don't you take off your coat, Daddy? I'll make coffee, okay? Okay?" she asked again when he didn't respond.

"Have to call my lawyer," he said, shaking his head. "Would you make some coffee, dear?" he threw over his shoulder as he wandered off to get his address book.

Becca roused herself enough to do the final dinner preparations. This was so lousy! If only she could call Mark and tell him not to come tonight. But she wanted him there — she needed an ally, someone stronger than herself. Of course, her father would be too distracted to do or say anything awful, and that was one comfort.

At five o'clock, she showered and washed her hair. She had chosen a favorite skirt-and-sweater outfit — cream-colored wool top and A-line skirt that showed off her slim figure. Somehow, even though she'd been eating as much as she normally did, her body had changed, and at least she looked like she'd lost a few unnecessary pounds. What was it Judy had said about baby fat? Even her face looked less chubby and babyish, she thought, as she smoothed on blusher and just a touch of mascara. She blew her hair dry and tied it back with a pink ribbon before putting on a pair of seed pearl earrings, her mother's last birthday present to her. Her thoughts flashed over the long, cold miles to Rachel. What was she doing tonight? Studying as usual? Entertaining her new college friends? Shaking the various possibilities from her mind, Becca stepped out of the bedroom and gingerly walked to her father's door. She took a breath and knocked.

"Yes," Dr. Walters answered quickly. "I'm coming. I know it's about time."

He threw open the door and stood smiling at her, a totally different man from the one she'd seen that morning. He now looked brisk and professional, as though he had just come from his rounds at the hospital. It was nothing short of amazing to Becca that he could turn his emotions on and off so efficiently. She was like an exposed nerve half the time, and could never hide what she felt.

"You look lovely, dear," he nodded approvingly, brushing absently at her shoulder. "But I think you could do with a haircut. What about it?"

"Yes, Daddy," she sighed, wondering why every compliment had to be accompanied by a criticism. Well, he'd had a rough day — she could forgive that.

"Now, what needs doing?" He walked her quickly to the kitchen, admiring the neatly laid table and the centerpiece of flowers as they passed through the dining room.

"It's pretty much under control. Just the salad dressing, I guess," Becca said.

"I'll take care of it." Her father moved toward the kitchen.

No sooner had he said that than the doorbell sounded. It was six on the nose. *Thank goodness he's on time,* Becca thought, small butterflies beginning a dance in her stomach. *Now please, may everything go all right.*

She threw open the door. "Hi!"

"Hi. Wow, don't you look great." Mark was carrying three yellow roses wrapped in tissue, which he handed to her with a flourish.

"Oh, Mark, how lovely! Thank you. Let me take your coat."

He had compromised about the suit, and he looked terrific. He was wearing a black turtleneck and gray wool slacks with a gray-and-blue heather tweed jacket over it. She particularly liked the navy suede elbow patches, which gave him the authority and class of a college professor. She was about to say something when her father appeared from the kitchen. Her stomach made a few rumbling noises as she presented the men to one another.

"Daddy, this is Mark Shuman. Mark, my father, Dr. David Walters." *Sounds like the beginning of a job interview.* She turned her back to hang Mark's coat in the closet.

"How do you do, sir?" Mark said, extending his hand. "I've been eager to meet you."

Don't overdo it! Her eyes flashed him a warning.

But her father smiled vaguely and shook the proffered hand. "Hello, Mark. I understand you and Becca work together."

"Yes, uh-huh. And we're both seniors at Halsted, but we hardly ever ran into each other there, for some reason."

Why are we all standing around? Why doesn't my father invite him to sit down? Becca had this picture of the three of them eating dinner right there in the hallway, holding their plates and shifting awkwardly from one foot to the other.

"How about something to drink?" She grabbed Mark by the hand and pulled him hastily into the living room. "Coke or 7-Up? I think there's some tomato juice, too."

"Coke would be great," Mark grinned, giving her that teasing look that clearly said, "Hey, it's no big deal — loosen up. Don't act like such a nerd."

"Daddy, what would you like? Wine or Scotch?"

"A little white wine would be nice, dear."

She practically ran into the kitchen to prepare the drinks. It would be disaster to leave them alone too long. Were they talking? Why couldn't she hear any voices? She turned up the flame under the chili and stuck a loaf of bread in the oven to heat. Then she fixed the drinks, giving her father an extra large goblet of wine in the hope that it might relax him.

She put the three glasses on a tray with a dish of nuts and brought them into the living room.

Her father was sitting uneasily in his big chair, and Mark was perched on a corner of the sofa as though he wasn't sure he was allowed to crush the cushions.

"Here we are!" she sang out cheerily, handing her father his drink before going to sit next to Mark.

"I was just telling your father how much I admired that painting." He pointed at the graceful figure of a ballet dancer posed with one pink toe shoe up on a stool.

"Yes, I like that, too, but this one is Daddy's favorite." Becca indicated another one, a rather somber abstract that reminded her of a stormy night in the city. The ballet dancer had been her mother's choice, and as soon as Rachel was out of the house, Dr. Walters had moved the dancer out of the bedroom.

"Are your parents interested in art?" her father asked, his gaze never leaving Mark's face.

"Uh, not really. I guess not. We've got a few nice posters, though." He shrugged noncommittally.

"I see." The doctor settled back in his chair with a frown, as if to show his disapproval of posters.

"My mother does wall hangings," Mark added. "Lots of rope and stuff. It's always lying around all over the place. You'd like it, Becca — it's weird," he laughed, turning to her.

"Really." Dr. Walters took a sip of his wine and Becca knew just what he was thinking. Posters instead of real paintings and a mother so sloppy she didn't even clean up after herself. *Oh, God, this is awful.*

"Mark is really an incredible technician, Daddy," she interjected. "At RFB, everyone is always coming to him when some machine is stuck. Why, just the other day —"

"I take it, though, that you don't intend to pursue this as a career?" her father asked anxiously.

"Fixing tape recorders? No, of course not."

"Ah. And what *are* your interests?"

Becca glared at her father. How dare he quiz her dinner guest like this! "Well, I think the food is ready," she said, jumping up and pulling Mark along with her. "Let's adjourn to the dining room. Mark, would you help me carry the dishes in?"

She dragged him into the kitchen and closed the door behind them. "I'm so sorry!" she began, but he cut her off.

"Hey," he whispered. "I'm having fun. I expected a grilling. You know, you always get that from parents. He's not so bad."

Becca sighed and handed him the salad bowl. "You're a brick, you know that?"

"Yup. Let's go beard the lion," he said brightly, taking the basket of bread and preceding her into the dining room. She took the chili casserole between two potholders, held her breath, and prayed.

"Daddy and I did this together," she said as she spooned out three heaping portions over rice. "We may open a restaurant some day, the way we're going."

"I hardly think that's likely, Becca. Restaurants are very risky ventures financially."

She shook her head in exasperation. "Daddy, I was only joking. I didn't really mean . . ." But then she shrugged, realizing that it was useless to protest. "Daddy sort of taught himself to cook when he was in medical school, but he's improved a lot since then."

"What about you, Mark? Does medical school interest you at all? Or is the law more to your liking? What field is your father in?"

Becca and Mark exchanged a quick look. "He's an accountant, sir. Well, actually, I haven't settled on anything definite. I think it'll be business, rather than being a doctor or lawyer. But that's all a long way down the pike. Becca, this food is magnificent. All of it, really — it's great."

"Where do you think you'll be applying to college?" Her father had raised his voice, and to Becca it sounded like a jackhammer, pounding away with one horrible accusatory question after another. *Tell him you're running away to join the circus!* she thought. *It'd serve him right.*

As if he could read her thoughts, Mark responded, "I'm not going to college right away, at least I don't think so."

"Oh?" Dr. Walters sat with his fork halfway to his mouth, one eyebrow raised in astonishment.

"You see, my folks and I have talked it over and, well, partly for financial reasons, we all thought it might work out if I got a taste of what I intend to do later. I figure I'll work for a year, and then — when I have my feet wet and know what'll be expected of me in the real world — then I'll take a crack at college and business school."

"Oh?"

Becca was squirming at her place. She was getting increasingly furious with her father and had to hold herself back from jumping in and defending Mark. Of course, he needed no defense. His plan seemed awfully sound to her. She was tempted to say she thought it a brilliant idea, that more people ought to do it, but her vocal cords were paralyzed. She still hadn't touched her chili.

"Wouldn't you imagine that freshmen of your own age might get a head start that you'll never have?" her father said thoughtfully. "It really seems to me that you'd have plenty of time to get used to the world of business after your schooling is finished. This way — you never know — you may get started and forget all about school. That could be a disaster."

"You may be right," Mark nodded, reaching for the casserole so he could take seconds. "And then, *I* may be right."

Becca wasn't sure how they ever made it through the rest of the evening, nor how Mark was consistently able to remain civil, even friendly, in the face of her father's apparent hostility. Because there was nothing else it could be. *He hates Mark!* Becca thought to herself as she brought in the coffee and dessert. *But he refuses to listen to him. He just makes pronouncements right and left.* She could feel herself about to speak so many times, and then a large invisible hand would clamp down on her shoulder.

Eventually it was ten-thirty, and Mark said he'd have to leave. Becca saw him to the door and handed him his coat. When he saw the distraught expression on her face, he reached for her hand and squeezed it.

"Hey, don't be like that. It's not the end of the world," he told her in a whisper.

"I'm not so sure."

"He's tough; he has opinions. I admire him for that."

"Then why doesn't he admire you for having your opinions?"

"Because, Becca, *I'm* a teenager."

She chuckled at that, and then he drew her close and kissed her lightly on the lips. She was so stunned she didn't have a chance to think about it. He opened the door and walked briskly to the elevator. "I'll call in the morning," he promised. The elevator arrived and the mechanical door clanked closed behind him. Becca took a deep breath and walked back into the apartment. Her father was sitting in the living room, reading the paper.

She stood in the doorway watching him, letting the whole series of events of that day and the many days that had gone before wash over her. Sure, he was going through a divorce, and that was lousy, but there was no excuse for his taking it out on other people.

"Well," she said at last.

He looked up in surprise. "Yes, dear?"

"I suppose you think it was a lovely evening," she began softly.

"I'm . . . well, I don't know. Your friend is a little, shall we say, immature?"

"*He's* immature!" Becca's mouth dropped open, and she took a step forward. She was boiling inside. "What do you call your interrogation of him? You think you have the right to sit and cross-examine my friends!"

"I was merely trying to determine whether he was an appropriate boy for you to date, Becca." He put his paper down and she could tell by the look in his eyes that he was angry. "I think that's a father's prerogative, don't you?"

She shook her head and walked over to stand in front of him. "Sure it is. But there are ways of doing that, Daddy, so the boy doesn't feel like an insect impaled on a pin. You wouldn't know what was appropriate for me if you fell over it!" Her voice was steady and she was amazed that she hadn't burst into tears. In the past, whenever she'd tried to confront her father, the enormity of what she was doing had opened the floodgates of shame and embarrassment.

"I think I'm able to use my judgment —"

"That's all you ever do is judge! If Sir Galahad walked in here, even he wouldn't pass the test. I'll tell you what it is," she added fiercely, her hands clutching the fabric of her skirt. "You're jealous! Nobody's as perfect as you! Nobody's good enough for me because you want me all to yourself!"

She stopped, gasping for breath. Her father was staring at her in shock. She had never spoken to him like this before. At first, she thought he was going to jump off the couch in a rage and order her to her room. She'd be prevented from seeing Mark ever again and would be grounded for at least three weeks. That was the scenario, she was certain. But she wouldn't give up — it was her right to say what was on her mind.

"Becca . . ." her father began. Then he sighed and leaned back on the sofa. She looked into his face and was astounded to see that there were tears in his eyes. "Oh, Becca," he murmured softly. "You're very hard on me, you know that?"

She was speechless, torn apart inside by what she'd done. He had been awful to Mark, but maybe he didn't know any other way to treat people. He'd always criticized her and her mother — it was sort of his way of challenging them to do better. It had never been something she'd enjoyed, of course, and she wasn't sure whether she did better or worse because of it.

"Well . . ." She stared at him and willed herself to remain in control of the situation. "You were pretty hard on him. I guess we could both be a little nicer."

"I suppose we could," he said.

Their eyes locked, but this time it was not in anger. Instead, they seemed to be searching one another for motives and answers. Becca saw herself mirrored in her father's gaze — she was his daughter, all right. He had given her the qualities of self-discipline and a sense of morality and all those things she lived by. If his standards were high, then so were hers. There was nothing wrong with having integrity and a notion of what was right or wrong. But maybe, she thought as she said good night and went into her room, maybe there was a middle course for both of them. For herself, she was going to try like the dickens to find it, and hoped like anything that her father would follow.

E^{ight}

The start of the Christmas season left Becca completely cold. The beautiful Fifth Avenue windows, the Salvation Army Santas with their uncooperative beards, the carols on Musak in all the stores and restaurants had, in years gone by, given her a thrill. Her parents had never really celebrated Chanukah or Christmas per se, but they did acknowledge the holiday season with presents. Becca loved the idea of a real Christmas, though, and she used to plan what she'd do when she had kids of her own. They would have a tree, of course, not a fake one but a sharp-scented fir, and the whole family would sit around and make their own decorations. Everyone would pitch in stringing cranberries and popcorn and drinking eggnog. Sort of corny, like in the commercials. Then on Christmas Eve, after the children were asleep, Becca and her husband, whoever he might be, would sneak out the presents and slip them under the tree, so that on Christmas morning, as early as they dared, the kids would be able to come downstairs and tear into their gifts. There was always a staircase in Becca's fantasy, since, as a lifelong apartment dweller, she'd never had stairs.

But this year, Christmas just seemed like a waste of time. It would mean a break from school and work — and just that many days when she couldn't be with Mark. The thought of Christmas Day at her Uncle Larry's house filled her with dread. Surely her Aunt Gert would ask about Rachel, and cluck over Becca as if she were an orphan or something. Her cousins, Jill and Laura, were okay, usually, unless their mother had them on some new project, like becoming Olympic ice skaters or winning the world's championship spelling competition. Gert was about the most competitive person Becca knew.

No, Christmas would just have to be endured, she decided as she walked into B.

Dalton to find a book for her father. They'd never made a big thing about exchanging presents — their big gifts were for birthdays only. Maybe a classy book and some ties or socks. He'd probably get her a subscription to *Time*, or something equally as juicy.

She wandered around the front of the store, past the best-sellers. It would be great to buy him one of those medical whodunits, but he'd never read anything as frivolous as that. Maybe a nice cookbook? These days he seemed happiest when he was concocting something delicious in the kitchen. But he enjoyed experimenting rather than strictly following recipes, so Becca vetoed the cookbook. She wandered on, past the flashy stands and special holiday displays to the more serious categories: history, politics, sociology, psychology.

I really should get him one of those books Judy's sister wanted to lend me. Something useful like Learning to Tolerate Your Teenager. *No, too didactic. We're trying to get away from that.*

She passed by the travel section. Then an idea hit her and she walked back, her eye caught by a beautiful picture book of Egypt, with extraordinary color plates of the pyramids and the Nile. Her father used to talk about a trip to Egypt; it had been his dream for years. But her mother only wanted to go back to Paris, city of lights and romance, where she'd made a brief excursion during her college days. Consequently, since they couldn't agree, they never went anywhere exotic, and vacations were limited to a week every summer on Cape Cod. Yes, the Egypt book was perfect for him.

Becca paid for it and pushed through the crowds to get out of the store and onto the avenue. A dusting of the first snow of the season lay on the tops of cars and on the wonderful angels in Rockefeller Center. She passed them and the gigantic tree behind them and she felt a little better. There were some nice things about this Christmas, actually.

She crossed the avenue and fought her way into Saks, quickly selecting three pairs of the navy socks she knew her father liked. She was on her way out again when a man's sweater on display at the next counter caught her attention. It was a hand-knit Irish fisherman's sweater, and the moment she saw it she knew it was Mark's. It practically had his name written on it. She argued with herself about buying it for only a minute; regardless of its high price, regardless of whether or not it was okay to give him such a personal gift, she had to get it. After all, she was making pretty good money. She could spend it any way she liked.

In Bloomingdale's, she bought a scarf for Judy, a soufflé mold for her aunt and uncle, and funny multicolored mittens and hats for her cousins. She went to an art supply store and bought her mother a fancy fountain pen and a bottle of violet ink. Then she started home, delighted to have completed her Christmas shopping so quickly and efficiently. The only thing nagging at her as she walked down the street was that she had spent more on Mark than she had on her father. *Well,* she rationalized, *he deserves it.*

The air was stingingly cold as she started up Lexington Avenue into the homebound crowds. There was something comforting about being part of a crowd, Becca thought. You lost your individuality and could be anything you wanted, at least for a while. She had a fantasy of stopping the well-dressed couple walking just ahead of her and pretending to be a tourist, lost in Manhattan. She was good at accents and that would add to her fun. "Ah *oui,* I am jhust 'ere from zee Sorbonne, you knaw?"

Becca, why don't you want to be yourself? She was suddenly very aware of her escapist tendencies. Always running from the truth, trying to mold things into an approximation of goodness. If she was good, if she did everything the way she was supposed to, then people would approve, would give her a pat on the back. She loved it when a teacher singled her out for a bright remark or a really excellent paper. *That's my problem,* she sighed, slowing her steps so as not to tread on the high heel of the woman just in front of her. *I want everybody to like me, and if they don't, I panic.*

Even Mark. Oh, she knew he enjoyed spending time with her, but what did he really think? She'd never had a boyfriend before, and guys had always been puzzling to her. They simply didn't think the same. They were enigmas, just as her father was. *Well, naturally, stupid, he's a guy, too.*

A chestnut vendor was selling nuts at the corner, and Becca, smelling the wonderful smoke from his cart, was immediately famished. She recalled vaguely that she hadn't eaten all day.

"Could I have a small bag, please?" she asked the elderly Hispanic vendor as she pulled her wallet out of her purse.

"You sure you want small, girlie? Is cold night," he offered cheerily.

"No, that's okay." She paid for the nuts and smiled. "Thanks. Merry Christmas."

The apartment was dark when she got there, so she had ample opportunity to wrap and hide her father's gifts before he came home.

She turned on the radio to her favorite classical station, got out wrapping paper and ribbon and scissors, and went to work. The announcer on the radio was pleased to inform her that for the next hour they would have an uninterrupted program of medieval and Renaissance carols, and Becca flopped down on the floor with a smile for her favorite period of music.

About fifteen minutes later, she heard the key in the lock. Her father hurried in, laden with packages.

"Well, hello! I didn't expect you home so soon." He was grinning broadly and seemed to be in a very good mood. Since the evening of the dinner party, he had been on his best behavior. Becca was trying hard, too.

"I didn't expect you, either. Lucky I hid everything."

"Oh? And what have we here?" He indicated the brightly wrapped gifts beside her.

"Some things for Judy and the cousins and Uncle Larry and Aunt Gert." She did not mention the sweater, which she had wrapped first.

"Uh-huh. Very nice."

"How about you?"

"Just some things."

"Very mysterious." She liked the fact that he wanted to surprise her. She might have expected him to ask her to make a list of things she wanted for the rest of her life and choose one a year.

"You can never tell from the shape of a

box, you know. Little things can come in big packages."

"Very sneaky!" She scrambled to her feet and took his shopping bags from him so he could shrug off his coat. He was in such a good mood, she almost felt brave enough to ask him something that had been on her mind for a week. Well, it couldn't hurt to mention it. But what if he said no?

"Now, tell me, who are Larry and Gert having this year? I hope their broker isn't coming — all those awful jokes he tells."

"No, I think they've given up on him. Well, Gert's mother will be there, if the weather isn't too bad, and she may bring her sister. You remember them?"

"Um. I was just a kid the last time I saw them. Hey, I've got a great idea!" She had to try it.

"Yes?" Her father began glancing through the pile of bills on his desk.

"Do you think Larry and Gert would mind if we brought Mark? There's always enough food to feed two armies, and Gert constantly complains about not having enough company up there in the country. Mark's parents celebrate Chanukah, so he's not doing anything special Christmas Day . . . so it would just be nice for everyone if we invited him, don't you agree?"

Her father pursed his lips and stroked his mustache. "You seem to have it all worked out."

"No, really, I was just thinking out loud. Oh, Daddy, please say yes."

"I don't know, Becca. It would be a little awkward. I'm sure Mark would feel out of place, since there would only be family there."

"Family! What family? We don't have any!"

"What a preposterous thing to say. You know what I mean —"

Becca raised her hands in an angry flash. "You're going to say Larry and Gert are family, right? Because they're blood relations. That's not what I call family. *My* definition is when people are close to each other and would do anything for one another. You know what we'll get from Gert? 'Oh, you poor thing, to be without a mother. David, how are you managing without a wife?' Not out of sympathy, Daddy — out of morbid curiosity. She's like that. She gets a kick out of other people's misery."

Her father let his breath out slowly. "So you'd feel better, more comfortable, if Mark were along?"

"It's partly that, I guess. Also, I think it would be more fun. For all of us." She gave him a look that begged for understanding.

"Well, I have mixed feelings about this, but

as you say, Gert can be difficult at times. And the one thing she loves to do is entertain, so I'm sure she wouldn't mind an extra guest."

"Then I can ask him?" Becca's eyes were shining. Maybe Christmas wouldn't be so bad after all.

He sighed. "Let me call them. Then you can ask him."

"Oh, thank you, Daddy." Spontaneously, she went to him and planted a resounding kiss on his cheek. He let out a nervous laugh and patted her head.

"Won't be the same as past holidays, and maybe that's not such a terrible thing."

She knew what he was thinking, of course. What was Rachel doing now? But Becca couldn't be bothered dwelling on that. It was far too late for regrets.

"Now," her father said with a sly grin, going over to retrieve one of his shopping bags, "I realize we still have two weeks to go, but you'd better examine this now, just in case it's not right and you want to change it." He extracted a large silver-wrapped box from the bag and handed it to her.

"But . . ." She was totally flustered. "Isn't it bad luck to open a present before Christmas Eve?"

"Under usual circumstances, yes. So we won't call this a Christmas present, because these are extraordinary circumstances. Go ahead now." He flicked his fingers impatiently. "Open it."

She nodded and removed the wide red ribbon before lifting the cover off the box. There, encased in layers of pink tissue paper, was the most gorgeous dress she'd ever seen. Slowly, she drew it out of its wrappings and just stared.

It was a soft, burgundy-colored knit with a rolled collar and dainty puffed sleeves that led down to tight buttoned cuffs. The bodice was a plain one of knife-pleated tucks, leading down to an elegantly simple, free-flowing skirt. Its self-belt ended in a bright silver buckle in the shape of a teardrop.

"I've never had anything so beautiful," she gasped, tearing her eyes from the dress to stare at her father. He was watching her closely, half-nervous, half-amused at her reaction.

"Is it your style?" he asked hastily. "I wasn't sure. And you'd better try it on to see if it fits."

The tag read SIZE 8. "How did you know my size?" she asked wonderingly.

"I looked through your closet," he said simply. "I hoped you wouldn't mind.

"Mind? Oh, Daddy, it's wonderful, just fantastic. I have to try it on." Leaving the wrappings all over the place, she ran to her room, unbuttoning her clothes as she went.

Did he do this to make up for that dinner party? she mused as she slipped the dress over her head. *Or is he just a nicer person than I give him credit for being?*

She examined herself in the mirror before going out to show her father. It was a perfect fit and maximized Becca's best features. The color warmed up her complexion; the cut flattered her figure. Her father saw at once when she went out to show him that he had made a fine selection.

"I bought it for you to wear on Christmas," he explained. "Wanted to make sure Larry and Gert knew I was taking good care of you."

"You are, Daddy," Becca said softly. "Honest, you are."

She raced to Mark's cubicle as soon as she got to work the next day. He was already busy transcribing a copy of a novel off a master.

"Hi!" she said brightly, leaning on the side wall. "How's everything?"

"Good," he nodded, still preoccupied with his work. "But looking forward to a week off. You know, you and I have been killing ourselves this semester." He paused to look up at her. "Busy this weekend?" he grinned.

"Only if you're taking me someplace." She finally felt easy enough with him to acknowledge in words that they were an item. It had taken Becca a long time to figure out that Mark really liked her, but she trusted that now, and didn't have to question his motives each time he asked her to do something with him.

"I will take you to *the* great Chinese fast-food restaurant of this city, lady. I will feed you the best Chinese fast food you ever ate," he smiled, returning to work.

"Super. And I will take you to Westchester on Christmas Day," she proclaimed triumphantly.

"Huh? What do you mean?"

"Remember I said we were going to my uncle's? And you said your folks don't celebrate Christmas, right?"

"Yes, but —"

"So, you'll be free and bored out of your mind. And you're invited with me and my father. Will you come?" She walked over and stood beside him, but he just frowned at her.

"No, thanks."

"How can you refuse? Mark, don't be silly. My aunt Gert makes the most phenomenal turkey stuffing with nuts and apricots and stuff. It's her secret formula. And my cousins are lots of laughs and my uncle is one of the sweetest guys you could ever meet."

"I said no way, Becca." He turned around to face her, and now he looked really annoyed.

"What's wrong?"

"Listen, I may be a real nice guy, but I'm not a masochist. I did your Face the Father act once; I don't intend to repeat it."

"It's not just my father, it's —" Becca began.

"Your father doesn't like me," Mark said.

Becca laughed at him. "What father ever liked his daughter's boyfriend?"

"Hey." Mark rubbed his forehead wearily. "You're looking for a patsy, to step in between you and Daddy while the two of you are carrying on this love/hate routine. I don't want the job."

Becca felt like he'd hit her. "It isn't true."

"Face it, Becca. That man has an incredible hold on you. Break it now or you never will."

"You're so wrong, you can't imagine." She whirled around and fought to hold the tears back. "I was just being considerate and asking you to a family gathering and you turn it into a federal case."

Mark shrugged. "I'm just trying to save my hide. See, contrary to popular opinion, I don't like being taken advantage of."

"Is that what you think I've been doing?" Becca stared at him aghast, her eyes brimming. "Mark, I'm not. I was just . . . I wanted to have you there because I like being with you and because . . ." She stopped, unable to go on with the truth.

"Because?" he prompted, refusing to let her off the hook.

"I get . . . I'm really lonely sometimes," she whispered.

He came over and gripped her by the shoulders, and then he pulled her against him. "We all are. But you can't use other people because it makes you feel better."

She cried in jerky, sobbing anguish into his chest. *Selfish, rotten, you ruin everything you touch,* she chastised herself. She didn't deserve him, she knew that now. Pulling away, she rubbed at her tears with her fists and started to leave.

"Becca!" Mark practically yelled at her. "Don't go off like that. You know, you're an idiot sometimes. I've never seen anyone so hell-bent on beating herself. Okay, all right, I'll go!" He threw up his hands in surrender.

"You'll . . . go? You mean, on Christmas?"

"Yeah, well, it can't be as bad as staying home with nothing to do," he grimaced. "Listen, I like being with you, too. I just think sometimes you don't see yourself too clearly, and then you act kind of weird. But if it's understood why you're dragging me along to a family celebration, then I'll come."

She tried to smile through her tears but didn't succeed very well. Then she realized how much he had to like her to tell her this. He was more perceptive than she'd ever imagined.

"I'm glad," were the only words she could choke out. But she was a lot more than glad.

*N*ine

The drive up to Mamaroneck was like a trip through fairyland. It had snowed heavily the previous day, and although the roads had been cleared, everything around them was white. The landscape was decorated with spun-glass icicles and shifting dunes of snow.

Becca sat between her father and Mark, playing with the dials on the car radio. "Nothing but country-western renditions of Christmas carols or rock 'n' roll. Yuk."

Mark smiled at her, and she knew he'd vote for the rock if it wasn't for her father. Both men had been rather cool when they greeted each other in front of Mark's house.

"It's that or football scores, I suppose," Dr. Walters sighed, turning onto the Saw Mill River Parkway. Becca snapped off the radio. "Would you get out that map, Becca? I never remember the exit number."

She giggled and explained to Mark, "We've only been up here about a hundred times since I was born. You see, I've inherited my dad's wonderful sense of direction."

"That's not fair," her father said in a mock-hurt tone. "Mark, she's terribly critical of me, don't you think?"

"Terribly. Hey, I've got an old buddy from camp who lives up near here. I know the area pretty well. Why don't you let me be navigator?" He nudged Becca in the ribs and she nodded without looking at him.

"Splendid idea, young man. If you can keep us from getting lost, I'll be forever grateful."

Becca looked curiously at her father. He seemed actually pleased to have Mark along for the ride, and what was even better, he was letting them both know it.

"Looks like Exit 7, how about that?" Mark asked.

Dr. Walters shrugged and pressed harder on the accelerator. "We can always turn around if we're wrong," he said confidently. "Beautiful day, isn't it? There's nothing like the shine of bright sun on the snow — I remember it from my internship days."

"That was up in Canada, wasn't it, sir?"

Dr. Walters glanced over at him, surprised that his daughter's friend would remember a thing like that. Becca could see a new appreciation for Mark growing in her father, and it did a lot to relax her. Despite her personal vow to stop trying so hard to please, it couldn't hurt for her father to like her boyfriend. Not one bit.

They arrived at one-fifteen exactly, only a quarter of an hour late. Uncle Larry was standing at the kitchen door, the smoke from his pipe wreathing his head like a ghostly crown. Becca ran from the car and he met her half-way, although he was only wearing a sweater vest over his plaid shirt.

"Uncle Larry!" She gave him a big hug and reached back for Mark's hand, to draw him into their circle. "This is Mark Shuman, and Mark, this is Larry Walters, my uncle."

"Thanks for having me, sir." Mark and Larry shook hands, and at that moment Becca's father joined them.

"You want me to have a patient on my hands? Larry, it's cold out here." The two brothers shook hands warmly and Larry clasped David Walters around the shoulders.

"How're you doin', kid? It's been a while."
They preceded Becca and Mark into the kitchen, and she watched them with a feeling of real tenderness.

"How are *you* doing?" Mark asked her softly as they walked to the door.

"Fine, really. It's just . . . so funny to hear someone calling your father 'kid,' you know? They haven't seen each other since the divorce," she added just as they went into the warm kitchen.

"Darling!" Becca's Aunt Gert dropped the spoon she was holding into a large pot and lunged at Becca, who submitted patiently to her effusive hug.

"You look marvelous, so lovely, just a little thin, doesn't she, Larry?" Gert enthused, helping Becca off with her coat. "This must be Mark, right? Well, we're terribly happy you could come. It's wonderful. Where are the girls? Girls!"

Two rather somber-looking cousins appeared at their mother's summons, one carrying a plate of olives, the other, taller one with glasses bearing an armload of presents.

"Hi!" said Jill, who was Becca's age minus a few months. She gave her a peck on the cheek and nodded to Mark. Becca watched her nervously pushing her glasses up on her nose and wondered what activities the poor girl was being forced into these days. Gert was hardest on her older daughter.

"Nice to see you," said Laura, the younger, chubby one who looked exactly like her father. She hardly glanced at Becca; her attention was riveted on Mark, and he seemed to like the scrutiny. Laura had just turned fourteen and had discovered boys overnight.

"Take their coats, give them a drink. David, you come here, I want to talk to you. Sit, sit!" Gert pointed to a chair at the kitchen table with one hand while she waved the young people away with the other.

Becca grabbed her father's hand and gave it a sympathetic squeeze before being rushed out of the room with Mark. Gert was evidently eager to get all the gruesome details of Rachel's awful behavior, but she didn't want to do it in front of the children. "Get him a large Scotch, Larry," was the last thing Becca heard before the swinging door promptly shut behind them.

"How've you been?" she asked Jill politely as they wandered into the living room. A roaring fire was the centerpiece of the room, and it showed off the antique furniture and fine paintings, each illuminated by its own spotlight, to good advantage. Everything was beautifully decorated for the holiday, although there was no tree. One thing Gert did well was run a house. *Unlike my mother*, Becca thought ruefully.

"Pretty good. School's okay this year. How about you?" Jill led them to the end of the room and deposited their presents in a heap on top of the ones already mounted up.

"Really good. I have a part-time job, you know. Mark and I both work at the Recording for the Blind."

"Oh, yeah?" Jill pushed her glasses up again, looking rather unhappy. How long would it be, Becca wondered, before her mother began pushing Jill to get some kind of classy job, just to be able to compare it to Becca's?

"Hey." Laura grinned at Mark. "You want the house tour?"

"I'd love it." Mark smiled, taking the ginger ale she offered him. "Becca's told me a lot about this place."

"Yeah, it's real historical," Laura giggled. "George Washington probably slept here, but he kinda slept around, if you know what I mean." She laughed hysterically at her own joke. "So, c'mon."

She led them through the elegant living room to the dining room, where a large crystal chandelier hung over the long rosewood table. There were twelve place settings, all perfectly laid out, with a sprig of mistletoe over the linen napkin at each place.

"Who else is coming?" Becca asked. "Anyone I know?" She was secretly glad there would be lots of people, because she didn't want Gert to have any opportunity to start in on her.

"Alice and Jimmy, the second cousins. They've got a new baby I haven't seen yet. And Grandma Druckman and her sister. They're okay, even though they're old," Laura assured Mark as her sister gave her a withering look. "Boy," Laura continued, "if I'd known you were coming, I woulda bought you a present." She took Mark's hand and led him up the stairs.

"Watch it," Jill cautioned him. "These are eighteenth-century steps."

Becca had always marveled at how tiny and narrow each step was, made for other people in centuries gone by. Her uncle's house was like a showcase, everything just so, and it had never felt comfortable to her. Even when her cousins were little, they were never allowed to go down to dinner before their mother had inspected their rooms and closets. The poor girls had spent half their childhood cleaning up.

Becca couldn't help comparing herself and the way she lived to her cousins in their fine home. As Laura dragged them from room to room, pointing out the low ceilings and the cedar closets, Becca counted herself very fortunate. She might be the victim of a difficult divorce, she might be lonely at times, but she was no mechanical doll to be dressed up and ordered about the way Jill and Laura were. It had always puzzled her that neither of them took after Larry, but then, Gert was the stronger force in the household.

Mark noticed the faraway look in her eyes and came over to prod her back to reality. "Suburban dream, right?" he whispered. "Not for us city kids."

"Uh-uh."

They heard the front door slam and Laura made a face. "Mom'll want us to play hostess. C'mon, Jill, before she yells."

The four of them trooped down the narrow stairs and back into the kitchen where Larry was helping the newcomers off with their coats.

"Darling, you look so wonderful," Gert was saying to her mother, a tiny lady about half Gert's size with perfectly immobile white hair.

"I'm cold, I'm not fine," she complained, scanning the room for a familiar face. "Is that Rebecca? Little Rebecca? Sarah, look at her, how she's grown into a beautiful young lady," she said to her sister, a considerably younger woman with dark red hair.

"It's been a long time," Becca acknowledged. "Mrs. Druckman, this is my friend, Mark Shuman."

At that point, another car pulled up, and out piled the second cousins, Alice and Jimmy. Their baby was swaddled in layers of blankets, and Alice hugged him to her chest as they trooped into the kitchen.

"Hello, everybody," Alice exclaimed, going over to kiss Gert. "Rebecca, I'd hardly know you. Hi, David."

"What are we standing around here for? You're in my way, Larry. Get everyone out and give them a drink, will you? How many times do I have to say it?" Gert began bustling again, her spoons clinking everywhere. The rich aroma of turkey dressing rose from the oven. "There's hors d'oeuvres, you know. I'm not trying to starve anyone. Go on!"

They hastily made way for Gert and went by twos and threes into the living room. Becca's Uncle Larry drew her into an embrace.

"How's my girl?" he whispered. "You look great. Nice dress."

"You should know — you're in the dress business," Becca chortled. "Actually, Daddy picked it out for me."

"He did! He never had that kind of good taste when he was married. What's gotten into him?" her uncle mused, looking across the room at David Walters.

Becca followed his glance and saw what Larry saw — her father, surrounded by the older people, making them comfortable, getting them plates of hors d'oeuvres and drinks. His face shone in the firelight; Becca could not ever remember seeing him this happy.

She'd been wrong to suggest they had no family — for her father, this was as close as he'd come in his lifetime. His sense of what it meant to be "related" was totally different from hers, and she knew that this sort of occasion closed the gap in his life. Not in hers, though. The person she most relied on in this group was not a relation, but he was something more to Becca.

The cousins were sorting the presents into different stacks, and Larry led her over to join them.

"Not everybody has something from everyone else, Grandma," Laura was explaining to Mrs. Druckman. "But we all have something, so maybe we should just dig in."

"You'll wait for your mother," her grandmother cautioned her, taking a deviled egg off her plate.

"Why don't I go see if I can help Gert do something?" Becca offered. "That way we'll get to the presents sooner. I hope you like yours," she added to Mark under her breath.

"Don't be long," he told her as she went back to the kitchen.

Gert seemed to be in three places at once. She was checking the turkey, putting the cranberry sauce into a dish, and giving the salad a final toss when Becca came in.

"I thought maybe you'd like an extra set of hands, Aunt Gert," she said.

"Feh!" Gert muttered. "You'd only get in my way. But I want to talk to you. Have a seat. Now, you're getting along all right, the two of you? Your father seeing anybody else yet? How are you managing the household?" She ran all her questions together so that they blended into one.

Becca gulped and shook her head. She should have known better than to find herself alone with this busybody. "We're fine, Aunt Gert. Both of us. The house looks great — never better."

"Well, I shouldn't wonder. *She* never took care of the house. He's going out with other people, is that right?"

"No, it's not!" Becca exploded. She bit her lip and forced herself to be calm. There was no reason to allow Gert room for assumptions. They were all likely to be false.

"We're learning to cook together. Actually, it's lots of fun."

"Fun!" Gert practically fell forward into the pot of peas on top of the stove. "She calls it fun! The poor child, the two of you, what a shame. The whole thing, such an embarrassment, so awful."

"Well," Becca said cheerily, vowing to end the conversation, "everything seems to be under control in here. It's a true fact, Aunt Gert," she went on, "no one can manage a dinner party like you. So why don't we go on inside?

They're champing at the bit to get into the presents — especially Laura."

"I suppose," Gert sighed, untying her apron and draping it over a chair. "Things could be worse," was her final comment as Becca finally coaxed her out of the kitchen and into the living room.

Laura and Mark were busy shaking boxes to see what was inside them when they came in.

"No, I'm telling you, the market's bad and there's nothing you can do about it," Mrs. Druckman's sister Sarah was saying to David Walters. "We've all been through a lot and what can we do but complain? Might as well just enjoy what we have, small though it may be." Her sister nodded vehemently and took a sip of her drink.

"That's a good philosophy," said Becca's father, giving his daughter a look that clearly said, "*So Gert got you, too.*" "Now, how about those presents?"

"Yay!" Laura yelled, making herself administrator of the piles of gaily wrapped boxes. "This is my favorite part. Oh, I hope I got hot rollers," she said pointedly to her mother, who ignored her.

"Jill, give Uncle David and Becca their present. This is for the two of you," Gert said, taking a thin envelope from her daughter. "You can use this. Well, open it."

Becca glanced up at her father in amusement as she ripped open the envelope. It was two gift certificates. One was for a rather posh Manhattan restaurant and the other was for a day's use of a home-cleaning service. This was evidently Gert's way of telling them they would surely starve and fall into rack and ruin without a woman around the house.

"Thanks, Gert, these are terrific." Becca grinned, going over to give her aunt a kiss. "Um, Daddy, these are for you." She picked up the two packages and handed them to her father.

When David Walters opened his book, Becca knew at once she'd made the right selection. His delighted expression clearly told her it was a thoughtful gift, one he would enjoy for years whenever his fantasies took him traveling to Egypt.

The cousins were presenting the older people with their gifts, so Becca took the opportunity to give Mark his sweater.

"Oh, Becca! This is too much. Hey, thanks!" He gave her a big bear hug and then shrugged off his jacket to try on the sweater. It fit perfectly, just as she had known it would. "I'll wear it forever," he promised, handing her a small box he had kept in his pocket. "For you," he said.

It was a delicate gold bracelet, and she

slipped it on at once. "Mark, it's gorgeous! You really know my taste," she whispered.

"All right, you two, all right," Uncle Larry interrupted them. "No mushy stuff in the living room. That's for later."

The presents were finally all opened, and the elegant room was littered with paper and ribbon. It was Becca's private opinion that it looked a lot better with a little confusion. Everyone was showing off their new items and talking at once. *It feels really nice to be a part of all this*, Becca thought to herself, mentally stepping out of the group and scanning the room.

"I think it's time to eat," Gert proclaimed, taking the baby from Alice. "Does Fred here get formula or what?"

"Gert, I'm breast-feeding. Come on, I'll just put him in the carrier and sit him next to me on a chair." Jimmy escorted his wife and child into the dining room and Becca and Mark were next in line.

"Any special seating?" Becca asked her aunt.

"Well, of course, it's boy/girl as much as possible, and you're not allowed to sit next to the man you came in with. David, I want you here, over by me." Gert gave him a push that sent him directly into the chair at the head of the table. "My husband, as you know, can't carve a bird to save his life. You're the surgeon, so it's your job."

"I haven't had surgery since I was an intern!" Becca's father laughed, but Larry gratefully took a seat at the far end of the table, leaving his brother at the head. Everyone jostled for a place and Becca found herself directly across from Mark. *Having fun?* she mouthed silently at him.

Super, he mouthed back. But there was no time for any more communication, because at that moment Gert brought the gigantic turkey in from the kitchen. There was a chorus of appreciative comments from everyone.

"Who's going to eat all that!" Mark exclaimed.

"Ma, it's prettier than *Better Homes and Gardens,*" Jill said dutifully.

"Gert, you've outdone yourself." Larry laughed. Then he turned to Becca and added in an undertone, "I say that every year."

Becca couldn't help giggling.

"Now, who wants what? Don't everyone say white meat." David Walters approached the bird carefully, looking for the best place to make an incision, his brow furrowed and his small mustache bristling above his pursed mouth. Becca knew that for her father even something like this was a job to be done perfectly. But today, somehow, she didn't mind his fussing and concentrating. This was his way of telling everyone how much he cared, how pleased he was to be chosen as king of the show. As she watched him at the head of the table, she was unaccountably proud. *I love him*, she thought suddenly, and unbidden tears sprang to her eyes. Loving him was not an easy thing to do.

"Uncle David, you better fill up those plates. Ma absolutely cannot abide leftovers," Laura announced.

"I like dark meat, Dr. Walters," Mark offered cheerfully. "Could I have a drumstick?"

Becca glanced at him and then back at her father. How odd it was, seeing them together like this. The two people closest to her in the world, yet they were nothing alike. It was so confusing, having more than one allegiance. Becca wondered, as she took the plate her Uncle Larry offered her, whether it would ever make sense.

"Becca, you look like you just lost your best friend!" Gert's grating voice brought her back to reality, and she picked up her fork, embarrassed.

"Don't be silly, Aunt Gert. I got something in my eye," she lied. Mark shot her a look of disbelief and she kicked him under the table.

"This is incredible, Gert," Alice exclaimed, reaching over to catch a dribble coming from

170

her baby's mouth.

"You're still the best cook in Westchester," David Walters exclaimed with a sigh of satisfaction.

"I know," was Gert's response.

"I would like to propose a toast," Becca's father went on, his happy gaze lighting on her. He raised his wine glass and everyone stopped eating to pick up their own glasses. "To a joyous New Year with lots of good companionship. And many family gatherings like this one."

"And that the market picks up," added Sarah.

Becca raised her glass along with everyone else, but silently, she made her own toast: *To the end of loneliness*. Then she smiled at her father and Mark and took a long, deep swallow.

Ten

The day after Christmas, as Becca and her father were enjoying a leisurely Monday morning breakfast, the doorbell rang. It was UPS, with a thin packing crate for Becca from Michigan.

"Sign here, please," the redheaded delivery man told her father while she tore into the crate with a hammer.

"Oh, Daddy, it must be Mom's Christmas present," she said excitedly. The box lay in pieces on the floor, and she attacked the next layer of wrapping — strips of padded tape.

At last the prize was uncovered. It was an oval mirror with a magnificent pewter Art Deco frame. The enclosed note read: *So you can see inside your soul. Love, Santa.*

"Isn't it gorgeous!" Becca exclaimed, holding the mirror up for her father's inspection.

"Expensive," was his assessment.

"I better go call her." Becca bundled up the wrappings and stuffed them in the crate, totally overwhelmed with her mother's generosity and good taste. Grasping her present carefully with both hands, she brought it into her bedroom and propped it up beside her as she dialed her mother.

"Hi, Mom!" She heard the long-distance crackle and her mother's sleepy hello on the other end of the line.

"It's so early, sweetie," she moaned. "What's up?"

"I just got the mirror and I love it," Becca said. "I had to tell you." She could picture her mother's lovely face as she spoke into the receiver, and all sorts of memories came back to her. She hadn't thought lately about their good times together, and she felt sort of guilty about that.

"I'm really glad you like it. I found it in this adorable antique shop outside of town. I was just tooling around one day and stumbled on it. Hey, and I loved your ritzy fountain pen.

It was the perfect gift for a struggling old student." Rachel's laughter gurgled through the phone wires like a rushing stream.

"Did you have a good Christmas, Mom?" Becca asked, determined not to mention how terrific hers had been.

"Christmas? What's that? Sweetie, I've been buried up to my ears in Community Relations and Family Dynamics. In just exactly one week and three hours, I will get to prove myself. Boy, I'd forgotten the pre-exam shakes."

"I know what you mean," Becca said with a wry chuckle. She realized, as she listened to her mother, that something was gone. She had lost that vague, spacy way of talking that included herself and no one else in the conversation. Becca wondered whether school was making her grow up, just as living alone with her father had done for Becca.

"We start the new term in a week and I'm expecting some real killer tests. I sympathize completely, Mom. Look, you better go to work. Study hard. And good luck. And thanks!" she yelled into the receiver. "I love the mirror."

"I knew it was you the second I saw it," Rachel told her. "Talk to you soon, baby. And Happy New Year."

"I hope it will be," Becca whispered as she hung up. She stared at herself in the mirror for a second, and then went in to join her father.

"This is it. End of the line." Judy swung her sheet of long blond hair and moved her tray along the rail. "I'll have the hot ham and cheese, please," she said to the woman behind the counter.

"What do you mean, end of the line?" Becca frowned and selected a fruit plate with cottage cheese. She'd eaten entirely too much over the holidays and was determined to look svelte again once spring rolled around.

"Dearheart, you have only five more months to be a high school girl. Then real life begins. Mrs. Schueler said some of the colleges even let you know in February on early admissions. That's for brains like you, of course. Me, they'll probably tell the day before freshmen have to go sign in. 'Okay, Miss Stern, we got a no-show, so I guess we gotta accept you. Congrats!'" She sighed and pushed her lunch tray to the end of the line, where she poured herself a cup of coffee and waited for Becca to catch up with her.

"What do you think your best shot is?" Judy asked her friend while they paid for their food and began to scan the cafeteria for empty seats.

"Hard to say," Becca muttered thoughtfully. "I'll never make Yale, and I don't think we can afford it, anyway, even though it's my first choice. Probably NYU or SUNY Purchase are more likely, unless for some reason San Francisco State says yes."

"Boy," Judy breathed, pushing over a discarded tray and taking a seat. "All the way to California! I'd never *see* you."

"Well . . ." Becca murmured, taking a bite of her lunch. She'd applied in the early fall when she would have done anything to get as far away from her father and New York as it was possible to get. At that point her first choice was the University of Mars. She had purposely not applied to Michigan, her mother's school. Her feelings about Rachel were a lot different now than they had been last September. And it was only at her father's insistence that she had reluctantly filled out the application for NYU. Even Yale in New Haven seemed perilously close then, not to mention expensive. SUNY Purchase was her safety application.

But now that things were humming along with Mark and her father was behaving like a human being, she saw no reason why she should go beyond her front door. The other weird thing was the thought of Mark not sharing the college experience with her, at least not for the first year. He'd been considering a variety of jobs, some of them through old friends of his parents in Ohio, where his mother had grown up. What would it be like without him? They were virtually inseparable these days. Each experience shared brought them closer, and sometimes it was uncanny how they would say the same thing at the exact same time. Becca had never had a best friend, and to have your boyfriend be your best friend was really more than any girl had a right to hope for.

Then there was her father. How could she leave him alone? It was one thing to abandon ship when she could barely say a civil word to him, but now that their relationship had changed, it was unthinkable. He would just rattle around in that empty apartment. Unless, of course, he had just been waiting for her to get out of the house before starting a real social life of his own. Becca suddenly had this picture of her father wearing a smoking jacket, uncorking a bottle of champagne while soft romantic music poured from the stereo system. She giggled at the idea and Judy looked up from her sandwich.

"You daydreaming again, dearheart?"

"Could be," Becca grinned, thinking she hardly ever allowed herself the luxury of daydreams now that her everyday life was so much more interesting. "Sort of thinking what it was going to be like, leaving home."

"For me, it will be sheer heaven. No pesky little sister, no older one parading around so immersed in being a college student she can't do her share of the chores. And no parents leaning over my shoulder every time I bring a boy home. You know what my real dream is, though?" She didn't wait for an answer but continued, "I've always been dying to stick my speakers out the window and blast the neighborhood with the Stones. At college, everyone does it!"

"I see your point," Becca nodded, although she didn't. She tried hard to dredge up at least one thing that would improve for her if she went away to college. Suppose San Francisco State was the only school she got into? Then she'd have no choice. She suddenly had an urge to go find Mark and pelt him with every thought running through her head. But at that moment the bell rang for the end of the period.

"C'mon, we'll be late," Judy said, polishing off her cup of coffee and scooping up her tray. "Can't wait to hear about America's socio-economic development after the Civil War, can you?"

Becca shook her head at her incorrigible friend. Maybe it was being the middle child of the family that made her so blasé about things. The youngest one got petted and spoiled; the oldest got criticized and worried about; and it fell to Judy to pick up the pieces. *Wasn't I lucky to be an only child*, Becca mused as they climbed the stairs to their fourth-period history class. *I got the whole ball of wax. Some good, some bad, but all mine.*

Their teacher, Mr. Rydell, was a favorite at Halsted High. He actually made history a living, breathing course of study. You were never bombarded with dull dates and battles with Mr. Rydell; instead, you got cause and effect. He was an exceptionally tall man, well over six feet, with a pale face and nearly invisible eyelashes, and he had a penchant for wearing white or cream-colored suits, even in the winter. When you saw him standing quietly in front of a blackboard, he looked like an enormous limestone pillar. Then he started to talk about history, and the obvious love he had for the subject animated his placid face and body until he looked like an entirely different person. Mark had him in another period, and he and Becca agreed that if more of their teachers were like Mr. Rydell, more kids would take learning seriously.

"All right, we were up to the Reconstruction, I believe. Miss Panter, would you take a seat, please?" Mr. Rydell was perched on the edge of his desk when Judy and Becca walked into the room, and he nodded to each of them as they sat in their assigned places. Becca couldn't help thinking that it was hard to distinguish the white chalk Mr. Rydell was holding from one of his fingers.

"I have an announcement, though, before we get going today, so I need everyone's attention, please." He frowned at Gail Panter, who was still fooling around, and she quickly popped into a vacant seat.

"Okay," he went on, "now it turns out that what I've been telling you for months is true, and I *do* have friends in high places. I'm *very* well connected."

A ripple of laughter ran through the classroom. He was forever dropping names in class and leading them to believe that somewhere in his past he had been friendly with Teddy Kennedy, Walter Mondale, and a variety of other political luminaries.

"I've been given the opportunity to take fifteen of my students — that's from all of my three senior classes — on a little trip to Washington, D.C., at the beginning of March. I tried to time it so you'd get to see the cherry blossoms, but sorry, the best I can do is get you in to see Kennedy, Tip O'Neill, and Justice Sandra O'Connor."

Everyone began talking at once. Was he kidding? Who would the fifteen be and how was he going to select them?

"Hey, quiet, you guys." He raised his hand for order. "This is a really special opportunity, but you're going to have to do a lot of homework if you want to be considered for the field trip. I don't want anybody sitting in some big senator's office and being ignorant of his voting record, okay?" He eased his large form off the desk and began walking around the room. "Now, here's what's going to happen. I've spoken to Mrs. Cioffi, and she's agreed to come as the other chaperon on this trip. Even though she's the expert in European history, she'll be happy to supervise this with me. And you'll be delighted to know that our principal, Mr. Woolcock, is letting those of you who go get out of your other classes for the week you'll be in Washington, as long as you make up every scrap of work by the end of the term."

Becca had almost chewed her pencil in half. She couldn't wait to talk to Mark about this. Wouldn't it be fantastic if they could both go? Her mind did flip-flops, taking her from the classroom to Capitol Hill. She'd get to hold hands with Mark at the Lincoln Memorial and the Washington Monument. Together they would meet the men and women who made policy and ran the country. Maybe they'd even get to say hello to the President!

"So, I'm assigning you in-depth coverage of *The New York Times* and *The Washington Post* for the next two weeks. There will be an essay exam at the end of that time which will give me the opportunity to see which of you clever devils have the best grasp of current events. Remember, only fifteen get picked, so the grading will be very hard. And now," he said, returning to the blackboard, "file that away. Miss Panter, what can you tell me about industrial development in the North after the Civil War?"

Becca floated through her next classes, unable to think of anything but the trip. It would be so neat to go with Mark. Well, why not? They were both good students, and even if she didn't read the paper from cover to cover every single day, she watched the news a lot on TV and was aware of what was happening in the country. She vowed to be totally diligent, to absorb current events into her pores, if necessary.

She got to work early that afternoon and was on her way to Mark's cubicle when Mrs. Samuels stopped her in the hall.

"Oh, Becca, have you seen Joanie?" she asked in a concerned tone. "She left the library a complete mess last night. I'm really upset."

"Uh, sorry, I just got here myself. You want me to straighten stuff up?" Becca was feeling so energized about the trip, she could probably have done the work of three that afternoon.

"No, it's her problem. Let me know if you see her." Mrs. Samuels marched stolidly down the corridor and Becca shrugged, turning back in the direction of Mark's cubicle. But she had no sooner gone two steps than she was nearly hit from behind by a whirlwind with Joanie's red hair flying in all directions.

"Oops, sorry. Really." She paused in her race and gasped for breath. "I meant to get here and clean up before she saw."

"Too late." Becca smiled sympathetically. "She's pretty burned." She couldn't help staring at Joanie. Something was different about her looks, about her whole manner. The terrified rabbit had metamorphosed into a much prettier, much healthier-looking girl. Becca was dying to comment on the change but was afraid she might drive her back into her shell.

"I'll apologize. I had an excuse, but . . ." She licked her lips nervously and seemed to be pondering the advisability of telling Becca the truth. "Someone came to pick me up last night, see, and I kind of left everything lying around. I'm not usually like that," she added, still glancing furtively down the hall for any sign of an approaching supervisor.

"I know you're not," said Becca encouragingly, walking beside her.

"I shouldn't say, but" — she lowered her voice to a breathy whisper — "I have a boyfriend." Then she turned completely red and looked at the floor.

"Why, Joanie, that's fantastic!" Becca burst out. Personally, she was astounded, but she didn't want to act like it was anything unusual.

"He's . . . oh Becca, he's so nice," she confided, diving for the stack of tapes still lying on the library reception desk. "He's coming for me again tonight, so maybe you can meet him. I hope you like him." She smiled broadly. "He's, well, he's a little shy."

"I bet he's terrific," Becca laughed, daring to reach over and pat Joanie's thin hand. "I'd love to meet him." She strolled happily past the library and the recording rooms, marveling to herself that someone as pathologically shy as Joanie could actually come far enough to the surface to talk to a boy. *I guess there's hope for all of us,* she mused as she rounded the corner and turned toward Mark's cubicle.

"Anybody home?" she sang out. He was on his hands and knees sorting tapes.

"Did you hear about the trip?" were the first words out of his mouth.

"Mark, we have to get picked. I know, let's quiz each other on the newspaper every night after work. One of us is bound to remember some stuff that doesn't stick with the other."

"Good idea. We can always use our work money for the train and hotel room if we make it."

"Mr. Rydell didn't even mention the financial part to our class." She sat on his desk and swung her legs back and forth in sheer, delirious joy.

"Yeah, we go down on Sunday evening on the train and we all check into a hotel. That's our base of operations. But he's arranged something so we get a break on a lot of our meals."

"Formal dinner with the First Lady in the White House?" she asked, giving him her best snooty expression.

"Geez, I hope not! But won't it be great to see the wheels of power grinding away? You know, the best thing about this trip is that whatever we learn we're going to remember. It's not like reading the stuff in a book," he enthused. "It's being part of the process — actually watching history being made."

"Whoa, boy, slow down." Becca grinned. "You haven't been dubbed one of the Fortunate Fifteen yet."

"I will be," Mark said with his typical self-assurance. It wasn't boasting, it was just his way of putting things in order in his mind. "But you, now that's another story."

Becca grimaced and put her hands on her hips. "Well, thanks a bunch for the vote of confidence."

"I didn't mean whether you'd be picked, dummy. That goes without saying. I was referring to your old man."

"What about him?"

"Oh, come on, you don't think he's going to allow his little baby princess to go wandering all over the globe all by her lonesome?" He gave a skeptical grunt and turned back to his work.

"Why shouldn't he? Besides, it's not like we're going alone. There'll be lots of us, and two teachers."

"I know this, you know this, but the mind of a protective parent is a very weird thing, Becca. Weird!" he repeated, wriggling his fingers at her.

"Look, Mark, will you get off his case?" Becca sputtered, trying not to get annoyed. "Ever since Christmas he's been really nice to you and —"

He raised his hands in surrender. "I don't know about you, but I have work to do. And I would never dream of coming between a girl and her father."

She glared at him, and was about to start yelling when she saw that look in his eye. He was teasing her.

"Don't say it," she sighed. "I'm taking this too personally."

"You hit it on the head," said Mark, going back to his tapes on the floor. "How about we walk home tonight?"

"See you later," she mumbled as she turned away. It was so hard to keep on an even keel, and she couldn't for the life of her say why. As soon as she had all her relationships neatly coded and filed in the right stacks, boom, one of them would pop up like a grinning jack-in-the-box, surprising her again. From being antagonistic and afraid of her father, she had gone to the other extreme. Now she defended him, whether he needed it or not. *Take a rest, Becca*, she yelled at herself silently as she went about her work.

She was calmer by six o'clock when she snapped off the recorder and made her notes on the back of the tape box. Only three more sessions and she'd be finished with Piaget. It was tough going, but she was really fascinated with the psychologist's work on how infants perceive the world. Sometimes she felt pretty infantile when it came to dealing with experience. Everything was so new, it was always a fresh challenge. That was great most of the time, but occasionally it left her with that empty, lonely feeling. *No*, she corrected herself as she got her coat from the closet and went to the front reception desk to lock up. *Not lonely, just alone.*

Mark was saying good night to Mr. Gormley when Becca came around the corner. She waved to him from down the corridor and then nearly jumped a yard when a small white face popped out of one of the recording studios.

"Joanie! You could give somebody a heart attack," she grumbled. "What's with you?"

"Sorry," the other girl sighed. "But I've been avoiding him all afternoon. I'm sure he wants to fire me for leaving the place a mess last night." Her voice was all breathy and anxious again.

Becca was going to say something sympathetic, but she was still full of her thoughts and ruminations about relationships and she couldn't stop the tirade that poured out of her. "You can't hide forever, Joanie, and doing one wrong thing is no grounds for execution. For heaven's sake, don't whine and snivel. You have to learn to stand up for yourself and not let people walk on top of you." She was chastising herself as well as Joanie, but the words seemed to make more sense to her when they weren't all bottled up in her head.

To her enormous surprise, Joanie smiled. "You're right. It's only . . . Becca, this is all new to me. It isn't easy, but I'm trying."

Becca felt her heart go out to this shy girl. "I know." She put her arms around her spontaneously and gave her a hug. Then they continued down the corridor together.

"You ready?" Mark flipped the light switch and opened the front door.

"Joanie, where's this, um, person who was supposed to pick you up?" Becca asked.

"I called him and told him to meet me uptown. I wanted to make sure I cleaned up tonight."

"Right. Well, some other time. Good night, now." Becca smiled at her.

"Good night." Mark and Becca watched her saunter down Sixty-eighth Street.

"Funny girl," Mark chuckled.

"I like her," Becca said staunchly.

"You would. Now, maybe we better go buy an evening paper. How about keeping file cards on special events, so we can follow up from one day to the next?"

"Sounds like a good idea." But Becca's mind wasn't really on Washington. She couldn't get over her own realization about being alone. It didn't seem half as bad; it didn't make her feel like a small speck of dust blown across the planet Earth. Instead, it was more like having her own personal time capsule, moving in tandem with those closest to her. She might float away from them, but she could always come back.

"But then again," Mark was saying, "Rydell may add in factors of past test scores and class participation. Knowing him, that would only be logical. Ever been to Washington?"

"Hmm? Oh, no, I haven't. I hear it's a great city, though."

"Absolutely," he nodded, taking her arm and walking up Lexington Avenue. It was a lovely night, quite warm for late January, and the rush hour traffic was just starting to thin out. "Hey, I had some other interesting news today."

"Oh?"

"You remember that former business partner of my father? The guy who split for California?"

"I think so."

"Well, I wrote him about my wanting to work next year, and he wrote back saying he had a good friend with his own small construction company who might have a place for me in the office. The great thing is, it's right near the university, so I could fit in a few courses probably, even if I did them at night."

"California?" Becca repeated.

"I haven't said yes to the Ohio offer yet, and it seems to me, well, why bury myself in the middle of the country, right? I mean, if I can't have my beloved New York, I could still have warm bodies and alert minds in L.A."

"Not from what I've heard," Becca laughed. "Not the 'alert minds' part, anyway." She was determined to keep this light. He hadn't said he was definitely going, after all, and who knows, she herself might end up in California.

The thought of leaving both her father and Mark at one time suddenly gripped her, tightening a steel band around her forehead. It wasn't fair, not when she'd just convinced herself how it was perfectly normal to be a person alone. But to lose both these precious people for maybe four years, not counting summers, that was too much.

"The sleepwalker, ladies and gentlemen,"

Mark announced. "Watch her make it through screeching taxis and rumbling buses without a blink of her eye."

"Oh, was I fading out?" She smiled sheepishly.

"You don't do it as much as you used to, but when you do, I feel real solitary. You go away to some other world, Becca, you know that? I miss you when you're gone."

There, in the middle of the sidewalk, they stopped walking and stared at one another, their fingers reaching out to intertwine. He pulled her closer and then she felt his warm breath on her chilled face. His eyes were kind and gentle, and she closed hers for fear of falling over with dizziness and joy. Then she felt their lips touch softly. She swayed against him, and his arms went around her. It was so good, she didn't want it to end. In the circle of his arms, she knew how much he cared, and what was even better, she knew that she was capable of giving to another human being. All her confused emotions honed in on that kiss, becoming clearer and sweeter with each second.

At last they leaned apart, but she still felt the impression of his lips on hers. It was a wonderful, vivid sensation, and any time she wanted to call it back to memory, she could. It was hers now, for keeps.

"I like you a lot, Becca," Mark whispered. "I like you a whole bunch."

"Me, too," she said shyly.

"Even if you're a flake sometimes," he teased.

She burst out laughing and started for him. He dodged around a mother pushing a stroller and put on a burst of speed, but she caught him at the corner. They linked arms, avoided a lurching taxi, and made it to the opposite side of the street, still laughing.

"How about those newspapers, huh?" Mark asked, steering her toward a kiosk a few steps away. "Don't say I never gave you anything." He shoved two papers into her arm and paid the vendor.

"How am I going to concentrate tonight?" she sighed, walking on beside him.

"Think of Washington," Mark suggested. "Not just the city, but the father of our country. You're an expert when it comes to fathers."

"Oh you!" she exclaimed, and the chase was on once more. She ran after him until she was too exhausted to take another step. Panting, they fell into each other's arms and stood there, clinging together. The noise of the city was nothing compared to the pounding of Becca's happy heart.

Eleven

"I cannot ever remember seeing you so absorbed in a newspaper, dear," her father remarked in an amused tone that evening.

"Huh? Oh, this is for something special at school," Becca grinned. "It's a secret right now, Daddy." She had decided she might jinx her chances by telling him. And somewhere, in the back of her head, Mark's words ate away at her confidence. Naturally, once she was picked, her father would be thrilled for her. But there was no sense in getting him all excited for nothing. If she were not selected — but, oh, how she prayed that she would be! — then she didn't have to mention it at all. This wasn't lying, she rationalized as she skipped over the weekend section and went directly to the hard news. It was just good sense.

Over the next week, there was a new kind of senior at Halsted High. The seventy-two students of Mr. Rydell's classes changed overnight into diligent, serious news-watchers. Even the ones who hated history were enthusiastic about the possibility of the Washington trip, so they buckled down as tightly as the best students, making the competition even stiffer.

"I don't know," Becca said to Mark one night as they took a break in his mother's white-on-white kitchen. "I thought we had a shot at this, but I'm getting nervous. There are an awful lot of brains who are determined they're going to Washington."

"Aren't *you* determined?" he asked casually, reaching across her sheaf of file cards for another oatmeal cookie.

"Sure I am, but you know, what finally hit home this morning when I started my *Times* was that the stuff in the paper is only the surface. You have to have background, you have to know what was happening last year and ten years ago to make sense of current events. And the stupid politicians keep changing! And is he going to concentrate more on foreign or domestic issues? Oh, it's such a bog!"

"Becca, I will never understand how you can take something that's basically simple and straightforward and turn it into Einstein's theory of relativity. You love to imagine the very worst that can happen. Me, I just take things as they present themselves. Believe me, there's no one in any of Rydell's classes who knows much more than you or me about what happened ten years ago. So ease up a little, will you?" He bent across the table and planted a kiss on her cheek.

"I know. You're usually right about me, but this time, it's different. I feel so dumb when I look at this stuff, like I have too much to learn and I never will." She sighed and took a sip of her now-cold cup of coffee. Then she looked at her watch. "Hey, I didn't realize it was almost ten. I better get going." She folded the newspaper and stood up, anxious to get out the door and down to the lobby before her father arrived.

"What's your hurry?" Mark asked, but then it was too late, because the downstairs buzzer started making a racket.

"Who can that be?" Mark's mother called from the living room. "Mark, is one of your other friends coming at this hour?"

"No, Mrs. Shuman," Becca said hastily with no small amount of chagrin. "It's my dad coming to pick me up."

Mark stared at her, his eyes narrowing suspiciously. "Why didn't you tell me your father was picking you up?"

"Why should I?" She plucked her coat off the back of the kitchen chair and put it on.

"I know why. Because I'm always ragging you about how smothering he is, right? You're a big girl, Becca. You can catch a cab by yourself."

"Mark, it's late at night. Things happen in the middle of New York City. It's not unusual for a father to be concerned, you know. He doesn't want me mugged or raped or anything."

"Look, neither do I," he said in exasperation. "I'm not blaming you for getting picked up. I just wonder why you were too embarrassed to tell me. I thought we were straight with one another, Becca."

She bit her lip and looked at the floor. It was true, she had been less than honest lately. First not telling her father about the trip, then neglecting to tell Mark that her father had agreed to these late study sessions only on the condition that he drive Becca home afterward. Why was she afraid of the truth if she was really sure that her relationship with her father had improved?

"I don't know why," she told Mark frankly. "I guess I thought you'd make fun of me."

But before Mark could say anything, his mother had pushed open the kitchen door and was showing Becca's father in. "Are you sure I can't offer you anything, Dr. Walters? Coffee or tea?"

"No, really, that's very kind. Becca, I see you're ready to leave?"

Why couldn't they stay? Why didn't he want to accept the Shumans' hospitality? Suddenly Becca felt cornered and saw that same look on her father's face. *It's just like the night Mark came to dinner,* she thought. *When we all stood around in the hallway and he was as unfriendly as he could be. Why in the name of heaven doesn't he like people?*

Sullenly, she picked up her things, said a quick thank you to Mr. and Mrs. Shuman, and told Mark she'd see him at work the next afternoon.

"I'll get us the *Times* tomorrow," Mark smiled, looking from Becca to her father. "We want to be sure we're set for the Washington trip."

Becca whirled on him, so upset she didn't know how to respond. He'd said it! It was almost as though he knew she hadn't told her father.

"What trip is that, dear?" Dr. Walters asked.

"Oh, I . . . come on, I'll tell you in the car. Good night, Mark," she practically spat at him.

All the way down in the elevator, her

thoughts churned and boiled to an incomprehensible mush. Now what was she going to do? Mr. Rydell's exam was still a week off, and she'd be all the more nervous about it if her father had vetoed the idea beforehand. But then she wondered, *Why should he?* Maybe Mark was right, and she was just fabricating more problems than actually existed.

They walked through the slushy streets to the car, and the unspoken question hung in the still air. Becca closed the door on the passenger side and waited for her father to turn on the ignition before speaking.

"Our history teacher is planning this trip to Washington, D.C., in early March for the best kids from his classes. Mark and I are working hard, studying up on current events for the test he's giving next week. See, he's only taking fifteen out of the seventy-two of us."

Silence. Dr. Walters turned up Park Avenue and his eyes did not leave the street in front of him.

"It's an incredible opportunity, really," Becca went on, her voice getting higher and faster in her anxiety. "Mr. Rydell — that's the teacher — has terrific connections. It won't be just a tour of the city, see. The kids who go are going to have meetings with senators, congressmen, even a Supreme Court justice. It's really a once-in-a-lifetime opportunity," she finished, finally daring to turn and look at his face.

Nothing. No expression whatsoever. She wished she could fathom just a little of what was going on in his mind. Was he angry at her, pleased for her, upset that she hadn't told him before? But he was impossible to read.

"It's not going to be a very expensive trip, either. Just the train ticket down and back and part of a hotel room for a week. Some of the meals are even free." *He doesn't care about that part*, she cautioned herself. *But what does he care about?*

Finally, he slowed to a stop for a red light and spoke. "When is your last day of school this spring?" he asked.

"Um. I'm not sure. June 20, I think." She didn't ask why he'd changed the subject. Obviously, he wasn't concerned about the Washington trip. Or else, he was too concerned.

The Saturday before the exam, Becca fairly floated home from her violin lesson. Ms. Claymore had decided she was ready to tackle one of her favorite pieces — Handel's Sonata in D for violin and piano. She had sight-read the difficult runs with unusual dexterity that morning, and her teacher had commented on how well she was doing.

"You'll never make the New York Philharmonic, Becca," the wry little woman told her, "but you're in control of the instrument now, not the other way around. I'm proud of you."

As Becca swung her case by her side on that bleak February afternoon, she couldn't help giving herself an additional pat on the back. It wasn't just her playing or her schoolwork, it was her whole life. She was in control now, as she never had been before, even prior to her parents' divorce. She understood herself and her feelings better, she didn't daydream nearly as much, and she had a wonderful boyfriend who really cared about her. Even her father's attitude toward her had changed. As for her mother, well, that was different, too. Rachel was no longer a dream or a fable. She was a real woman with her own problems, and when she was part of Becca's life again, they'd probably have to deal with some of them together.

Her father was in the kitchen marinating a steak when she walked in, and he dropped a Worcestershire-scented kiss on her head when she came over to him, smiling.

"Have a good lesson, dear?"

"Great. I got that piece I wanted."

"The difficult one you mentioned? You'll have to put in some additional hours if you intend to master it."

"I know." She opened the refrigerator and

pounced on some cold chicken, left over from the night before. "No house calls today?"

"Not a one. Everyone's well, alas." Dr. Walters gave a short laugh and went back to peppering the steak.

"What are these?" Holding a chicken leg to her mouth, she picked up some brightly colored brochures that were lying on the opposite counter. Cheery scenes of sandy beaches, attractive shops, and overdecorated motel rooms greeted her eye.

"Travel folders. I'm planning a vacation," her father said smugly, covering the Pyrex dish with a sheet of wax paper.

"Well, you haven't been anywhere in a while," Becca said slowly, wondering what was going on.

"I don't think we can afford Egypt this time, what with my additional expenses this year" —he cleared his throat and Becca knew he was referring to Rachel's alimony payments— "but maybe a quick jaunt to the West or down South. There's a lot to see, right in your own backyard, you know. And there are excellent tours all over the United States."

"You mean, a vacation for you and me?" she asked incredulously, putting down her half-eaten chicken.

"Who else?"

"Well, I just thought . . ."

"What is it, dear?"

"No, nothing." She glanced down at the floor with a sinking feeling that traveled from her constricted throat right down to her feet. She hadn't thought much about the coming summer, but it would be her last chance to spend any time with Mark, depending on where their fortunes took them the following September. They hadn't talked about it, but Becca had simply assumed that they would explore New York, take long walks in Central Park, see hundreds of movies, and generally never leave each other's side. But her father could change all that with one slick, commercial brochure.

Becca couldn't tackle the problem right away; she needed time to think. "Let me know when it turns into dinner," she said, picking up her things and hurrying out of the room. "I have to study for my exam."

She spent every waking minute until the test on current events, and she even had a dream the night before about the Secretary of Defense. In the dream, he called her up and asked for her opinion about a top-secret weapon the government wanted to test out. She recalled that she had felt very privileged that such an important decision should be placed in her hands, and had dressed quickly so that she would arrive at the meeting on time. When she got to the well-hidden conference room, she found herself staring up at a group of the most gigantic men she'd ever seen. She was like Alice in Wonderland, having just eaten the cake that made her shrink. She peered up at them, unable to see past their belts. But the Secretary of Defense kept insisting that she examine this top-secret weapon, and she kept crawling around, trying to put herself in the right perspective so that she could get a glimpse of the whole thing. But it was impossible — she could only make out disjointed pieces.

She woke, sweating, the bedclothes a total mess. *What was that all about?* she asked herself, but it seemed too complicated to remember, so she let it roll out of her consciousness. Whatever it was, it had to do with her anxiety about the test, that was certain.

She and Judy skipped lunch and ate candy bars in their homeroom so that they would have every last minute available to study. And at two P.M. on the dot, they settled themselves behind their desks in Mr. Rydell's class and took the xeroxed paper he handed them.

There were three essays, one more difficult than the next. There was one on the economy — Becca's least favorite, one on foreign policy, and one on the United States presidency over the past twenty years. They were supposed to tie their ideas on the first two subjects into the third, which made the whole thing even harder.

Becca wrote until her hand cramped, thinking furiously fast, determined to drag in every opinion of every senator or congressman she could remember. At the end of the hour, she had filled three blue books and she was exhausted. But she had certainly done her best, and a wave of relief coursed through her as she walked out the door on her way to French. The good thing about this test was that it had really forced her to learn something, unlike most exams which generally only showed what the teacher thought was important. Whether she got to go to Washington or not, she had accomplished something.

"How do you think you did?" Mark asked when they met downstairs at the end of the day.

"Hard to tell. It was pretty tough. I sure wrote a lot — I just hope it was what he wants to read."

Mark looped an arm around her shoulder and gave her a squeeze. "Mine could have been tomorrow's edition of the *Times*. Well, we'll know soon enough. He's posting the names Monday morning."

The instant she got off the phone with Judy on Sunday, the thing rang again. She'd been glued to the receiver ever since Friday, and at least four kids in her class had called to commiserate about the exam after she'd made several of her own calls. She picked up the phone and switched to the other ear.

"Hello?"

"Sweetheart, it's me!" Rachel's voice sounded very close today for some reason.

"Mom, how are you?"

"Great. I aced three of my exams and did pretty well in the fourth, so I'm sailing today," she bragged.

"Hey, I'm proud of you," Becca smiled. "I'm just waiting for the results of a toughie myself."

"I'll keep my fingers crossed. Hey, sweetie, I was just thinking maybe we could firm up our plans for your visit now. I really want to show you Ann Arbor. Now, we have a whole study week off in the beginning of March, which would be really better for me than Easter."

"Oh, Mom." Becca looked at the phone in dismay.

"Your father could write you a note, couldn't he? And just ship you out here on a plane. You wouldn't miss that much school, and —"

"But you don't understand," Becca interrupted. "There's this class trip, and if I'm picked, I'm definitely going. That's the first week in March."

"Becca! C'mon, sweetie! I haven't seen you since before my hair turned gray, or something. It seems that long, anyway. It's really the only good time for me. Please."

"Mom, I can't. I mean, I don't think so. Please don't make it hard on me. I want to see you, too, but . . ." She felt torn in so many directions, and she hadn't really allotted time for her mother at all. If she suggested the summer, that might conflict with this vacation her father was planning for them. And when would she get time to be with Mark?

"You really can't forego this trip?" Her mother sounded like a hurt child. "We'll have such fun."

"Listen," Becca said in desperation. "There's a chance I won't be picked, in which case I'd love to come." That was the truth; it was just that she could see herself sulking around for that week, angry that she wasn't in Washington. No, she wouldn't do that, she vowed silently. After all, she did want to see Rachel. "If that doesn't work out, we'll make time this summer, when school's out for both of us. Okay?"

Her mother sighed and when she spoke again, she sounded less petulant. "I guess that sounds good. Let me know, all right?"

"As soon as I know, I promise. 'Bye, Mom."

" 'Bye."

There it was. The hard facts of life surrounded Becca, menacing her. How did you spread yourself thin enough to satisfy everyone and still take care of yourself? She wished she could think of an answer.

When Becca made her feet take her to the bulletin board after that long weekend of nail-biting and telephone conversations, she couldn't even get near enough to see the list. A crowd of seventy had beat her to it, and she stood on the outskirts, shuffling from one foot to the other. Every once in a while, someone in the group would cheer and someone else would curse. Eventually, the group started thinning out and Becca pushed herself forward.

"You made it, you lucky stiff," Judy said with a sigh, easing herself from the circle. "I guess I'm not cut out for politics."

Becca's heart started zooming around inside her chest, and it was hard to give her friend a sober, consoling word of sympathy. But as soon as Judy had gone, she plastered herself up against the board. There it was! *Becca Walters* at the bottom of the list. And what made it even better was that *Mark Shuman* was typed directly above it.

Going about the dull routine of the day was difficult, and waiting until it was time for Mr.

Rydell's class seemed ridiculous. The six kids selected from her group were given a variety of instruction sheets and a parental permission slip to get signed. Money for traveling and room and board was due in a week.

"Hey, you smart, beautiful thing, you!" Mark exclaimed when he finally caught up with her at the end of the day.

"Hello, genius. But of course you knew you'd get picked." She grinned.

"I wouldn't have gone without you," he said gallantly.

"It's touching, really." Becca felt as though spring had arrived overnight. Everything was perfect now. She couldn't remember ever feeling so good.

That night she nearly collided with her father, who was walking into the apartment house at exactly the same instant, and they both laughed as he gave her a peck on the cheek and asked how her day had gone.

"Oh, fantastic, Daddy!" She smiled, ringing for the elevator. "I got a big fat A on my history exam."

"Excellent. I'd like to see those in all your courses."

Tell him now, she prodded herself when they stepped out on the fourth floor. He put the key in the lock, humming, and she was relieved to see that he was in a good mood. *Go on, tell him.*

"I wish Mrs. Parkhurst would turn off these lights," her father said, dropping the mail on the hall table. "Electricity doesn't grow on trees."

"Uh-uh. I'll do dinner tonight," she offered.

"All right, dear. Thank you."

She looked at his neat blue pinstriped suit and maroon tie and thought about complimenting him on his appearance. *But I never do that*, she cautioned herself. *He'll know something's up. I just have to tell him, flat out.*

"This A on the history test wasn't just any A, you know. It was the requirement for the Washington trip."

Dr. Walters looked up from the bills and smoothed his mustache. "Trip? Oh, I believe you did mention something about that."

"I was picked, Daddy," Becca said, "and there were only fifteen of us out of seventy-two. Isn't that something?"

"Oh? Is Mark going, too?"

"Yes. Well, I never had any doubt about him getting to go, because he's a real brain."

"I see." A thin layer of frost had formed over his words.

"It's okay, isn't it? I mean, the trip is hardly going to cost anything and it's going to be an experience I'll never forget."

"Oh." Her father sighed and sat in his desk chair. "I'll give it some thought."

"But Daddy, I have to let them know immediately. And they need a deposit, and if I said I wasn't going I'd probably be laughed out of school!" She sensed something huge growing inside her, a bomb ticking away on a short fuse.

"Becca, I've allowed you a great deal of freedom this past semester, perhaps more than I should have. But you've never been away from home without your parents, and I honestly don't think it's being overly strict to say I don't want you traipsing off on some junket with your boyfriend."

Becca's eyes widened and she gripped the side of the desk. "Now just a second," she began evenly. "This is not a junket. It's a chaperoned trip with two teachers and the boys and girls are staying on different floors of the hotel. It's not going to be one long, wild party, if that's what you're implying. I thought I told you, we're going to meet important people, see government in action, and I —"

He was shaking his head when he interrupted her. "There are plenty of opportunities to do things like that. Do you know that if you write directly to a particular politician, he can arrange these in-depth discussions and private trips to Capitol Hill and the Supreme Court? I think it would be very nice if you and I went down there when school is over. We could see Washington, and then maybe drive down to

New Orleans. And of course, Fripp Island is just a plane ride away from South Carolina. I think those two different cities and a week on a beautiful beach might be just the ticket."

"So that's what those brochures were for!" she exploded, the rage about to take over. "It's a bribe, so I don't feel too bad about your not letting me go on the trip. I can't believe this!"

She clenched her fists at her side and glared at him with steely hatred. Why had she conned herself into thinking that anything had changed? He was still the same monster, still as cold and unresponsive as ever. He'd fooled her with cooking and the red dress and being nice to Mark at Christmas. He'd allowed her to believe she was in control. But naturally, he was an adult and she was still a stupid kid, and that would never change, not even when she was forty. He'd be an overprotective, smothering father until the day he died.

"I frankly think, Becca, that you'd get more out of a real vacation than some class trip. Particularly since we'd see and do the exact same things you've described. And surely the accommodations would be better, and we'd be able to fly instead of take a train. Maybe do a little shopping and sightseeing and —"

"*No!* Oh, no, we won't. Don't you see that I want to be with my friends, that that's part of the whole thing? I don't want to go shopping."

"I understand that you and Mark care for one another, but a week away from your parents together seems inadvisable."

"It's not just Mark! For heaven's sake," she yelled at her father. "You either aren't hearing me or you simply don't know what kind of person I am. I'm not you! The things you like aren't necessarily the things I like. I need room, Daddy. You've got to give me some room!"

It was nearly impossible to get the words out and yet they kept coming, giving her no chance to breathe. "You simply don't know how to let go. You're no father, you're a jailer. You wouldn't know how to behave with a teenager if they'd taught you in medical school."

Her anger was fueled by hearing the words she had never before been able to speak. And her father's reaction was total shock, as though he were watching his meek, mild daughter change into a fire-breathing dragon before his eyes.

"What do you expect of me?" he asked quietly, really wanting to know. "A parent has to set up limitations and boundaries for a child, just the way he does for himself."

"But your life is *all* limitations, that's the point!" she yelled. "You have no fun, no friends, you never do anything spontaneously. You're critical of me and you never praise anything I do, and damn it, I want some credit! I want to be treated like a grown-up."

He glared at her, his humble acceptance dissolving. "All right, that's enough now. It is not your place, young lady, to instruct me in how to act. I don't like your attitude."

She couldn't back down now. There were so many things that had been unsaid for too long, and now a lot of messy emotion oozed all over the place. "I used to go tiptoeing around this house, praying you wouldn't notice me and find something, anything, to pick on. I was so afraid of you jumping on me and my friends, I just shrank back into the wallpaper. I never stood up for myself. But I'm not afraid anymore, and you're going to hear this!"

"Becca, go to your room!" he shouted, and she could tell by his face that finally she had gone too far. "I don't want to hear another word. I make the rules around here, and whether you like it or not, you do what I say. I'm frankly not interested in your opinion of me, nor am I interested in continuing this conversation."

"All right!" she screamed. Whirling on him with a sob, she ran from the room and slammed her bedroom door behind her. The room spun; she couldn't stand up anymore. The weight of everything pressing on her was too great. She slumped on the bed, letting her tears spill onto the pillow, not caring whether he heard or not. *I hate him,* she thought. *He is an ogre. He's everything I ever imagined him to be.*

She clutched the pillow to her chest and moaned, so miserable she actually wanted to keep on crying because it would show her — and him — just how awful the situation was. She relished her pain and hugged it to her along with the pillow. *I have no parents*, she told herself. *They're both gone now, and I have to take care of myself.*

It took her an hour to cry herself to sleep, and only once during that time did she wonder how her father was feeling.

Rotten, she hoped.

*T*welve

The clock on the night table read seven-thirty.
Becca pried her swollen lids apart and turned
over, wishing she could fall asleep again and
stay that way. Her head felt like it was stuffed
with hot, wet rags, and her face was puffy from
crying.

There was no way she could face him. She'd
wait until he'd left for the office before she
came out. She'd be late to school — so what?
Maybe she wouldn't go at all. She'd never
played hooky before, and this was as good a
time as any to start.

She lay very still, listening for sounds, but

it was eerily silent. Perhaps he'd left already, wanting to avoid her just as much as she did him. She stuck a leg out of bed and eased herself up to a sitting position. It seemed silly, just hiding in here. Hadn't she sworn to herself that she wasn't afraid anymore? She could take it — she could take it all.

She threw on her robe and opened her bedroom door. All quiet on the western front. Without looking down the corridor, she made a dash for her bathroom and shut the door behind her.

Her image in the mirror thoroughly disgusted her. The Becca who had become so much more attractive over the past few months was gone, and in her place was a lumpy, white, angry mess of a girl. There was no way she would look normal enough to go to school today, absolutely none. She ran the shower as hot as she could take it and washed herself vigorously, scrubbing her back with the stiff-bristled brush as though it were a punishment. When she had dried herself off, she ducked back into the bedroom and dressed hastily in jeans, loafers, and a blue-and-black plaid shirt with a black vest over it. She tied her hair back in a bunch at the base of her neck.

Lying on her dresser, next to her hairbrush, was the parental permission slip. She smoothed the crumpled paper and stared at the wobbly words typed there. Maybe she'd forge his signature and go, anyway. It would serve him right. And when she got to Washington, she wouldn't even call.

No, you won't, she told herself resignedly, sticking the paper absently in her back pocket. *That takes guts. Something you don't have.*

She decided, after a last glance in the mirror, that she was ready to face the day, no matter what it offered. She'd just turn herself off to it, and nothing would be able to penetrate her shell.

But she still wasn't prepared for the sight of her father, sitting at the kitchen table, staring into his cup of black coffee. She noticed the glint of silver in his brown hair reflected in the overhead light, and it caused her a pang of regret. *He's getting older; he has no one but you. You're a real louse sometimes.* This refrain ran through her head several times before she tuned it out.

Walking unsteadily, she went to the refrigerator and removed the bottle of orange juice and a loaf of rye bread. She said nothing as she poured herself juice and put the top slice of bread in the toaster. Her father didn't look up as she drank her juice and got herself a mug for coffee from the cabinet beside the sink.

Why doesn't he talk or look at me or yell at me? she wondered, but her own lips wouldn't move. She stood beside the toaster and watched the clock on the wall. *He'll go soon,* she promised herself.

"We're down to the last of the milk. I'll get some more on my way home." David Walters's voice resounded in the quiet kitchen.

What a dumb thing to say, she thought.

"Oh?" She poured her coffee and sipped at the black brew. The noise of the toaster popping made her jump. "Damn," she muttered.

"I wish you'd curb yourself from that swearing," her father said. "What happened?"

"Burned." She threw the blackened piece in the garbage and didn't bother getting another. *Now what?* she agonized. *Somebody better say something quick. You would, if you weren't such a coward.*

"Listen, Daddy." She took her coffee and stood in back of his chair. "I just want to tell you —"

"No, I'll tell you." He turned around. His face was a white mask and he looked weary, as though he hadn't slept at all the night before. "I realize it's not easy for you. The divorce has taken a real toll, that's clear enough. You and I have some problems. I've been thinking about them for the past eight hours. I never, do you hear me, *never* want a repetition of that scene last night. Do you understand me?"

"Yes, Daddy," she murmured, the hostility

welling up again inside her. Fine, if he wasn't going to let her talk, she'd just keep it all inside, all her hate and rage and pain.

"I realize," he continued, "that there are times when we don't . . . communicate very well. I'm not an easy person to talk to, according to you."

She was silent, not daring to agree.

"If I set up restrictions for you, well, it's because that's what I think is best for you. I don't intend to . . . to . . . uh, cramp your style." He tripped over the colloquial phrase and Becca nearly laughed.

"But as to that trip, I don't see it. I would be surprised to see the other parents giving permission, but frankly, I'm not going to be led by others in this. Do you see any reason why you should go? Tell me."

Was he honestly asking her opinion? And what difference did that make if he wouldn't change his mind? She sidled into the other kitchen chair. "You don't really care what I think," she said evenly.

"Yes, I do."

"No, it doesn't penetrate when I talk to you, so what's the use?"

"That's absurd. I listen very carefully, believe me. I hear —"

"You hear whatever you want to!" she exploded. "Whether it's about the boy I'm dating or my schoolwork or my music or anything. It doesn't matter what I say, because of the way you interpret it."

"And I suppose you feel you have the right to criticize me?" He was really fuming now, his teeth tightly clenched over the words.

"Well, you do it to me. And now I'm asking for a little equal time, that's all. What do you think is going to happen on this trip that's so awful? You think it's going to be a damn orgy?"

"I told you to stop swearing!"

"Oh, this is dumb. I hate this." She got up and jerked away from the table.

"Becca, I don't like your hostility. I've never seen you behave in such a manner, and I'm seriously worried."

"You see?" She pounded her fist on the table. "It's silly to argue. You're the boss; I'm the little kid. I do what you want."

Her father got up to fill the kettle. He stood at the sink, his head bowed, his jaw working with frustration and impotent sadness. "I think we could use another pot of coffee. We're going to be here for a while."

"But, I —" Becca looked at the clock in panic. Suddenly she wanted nothing more than to get out of the room, and fast.

"So you'll be late. I don't have any patients till eleven. I think it's crucial that we talk." He turned to her and his expression was as open as she'd ever seen it. "What do you think?"

"Okay," she answered reluctantly. She wasn't quite sure what she was letting herself in for, but she did realize that this might be the most important discussion of her life.

They talked for over an hour, bringing up topics painful to both of them. They were hesitant at first, scared to death of saying the wrong thing. They took little baby steps toward each other and stopped before the finish line. But by the time the second pot of coffee was gone, they had begun to approach the truth.

"You see," her father said eventually with a deep sigh, "I'd like you to understand my perspective. No one ever prepared me for this." He glanced around the kitchen. "When you were growing up, I never suspected I might have to —"

"Take care of me?" Becca finished for him. "But you never wanted to!"

"I never had the chance. Well, all right, maybe I didn't try to butt in when I could have. But she was so close to you. I don't know, I guess I never thought I'd end up being a mother as well as a father."

"You were all along, though," Becca murmured quietly.

"What do you mean?"

"She was . . . Rachel wasn't so much a mother as another kid in the house." Becca blushed in embarrassment as she remembered. "We used to pretend we'd run away and join the circus together. Well, that was when I was *really* young. It was just something she said to be silly, but I suppose it made me feel it was us against you. Boy" — she shook her head — "was I wrong!"

Her father shifted uncomfortably in his seat. "Maybe I treated her like a child because it was easier for me."

"But she liked that!" Becca pointed out. "And I really think she got a kick out of her own routines — they were sort of for effect, anyway."

"What . . . what did you think of me when you were growing up?" he asked her earnestly.

"I thought you were . . ." Becca searched for a word. "You were the metronome that kept the world ticking." She laughed. "That's not an awfully nice image, I guess, is it?"

"Pretty mechanical." Her father laughed, and soon she joined in. "Was I that bad? *Am* I that bad?"

She winced, because it was very clear than even though he was laughing, this hurt him more than anything. Maybe she should stop the confessions and honesty and say what she thought he wanted her to say. But no, that would just land them right back where they were before.

"You're not deliberately mean, ever . . ." she began. "It's just that I can't take your protectiveness and your criticism all the time."

"I don't think I'm that critical," he said defensively, his voice suddenly harder.

"You see, you're doing it again!" She threw up her hands. "I try to get through and you cut me off at the pass."

"That's the way you see it, Becca. If I allowed you, you'd be running around the streets like a wild punk or something. I have to keep order."

"Order!" she scoffed.

"Becca, you had a very confused childhood. You had a mother who permitted you everything. And too often, because it was simply not my way to cause a scene, I allowed her the liberty to spoil you."

"My mother spoil me?" Becca looked at him incredulously, a gleam of an idea flashing at the back of her brain. "She did what she wanted and I was a convenient excuse. She might have spoiled herself, but I really wouldn't say she gave me any more freedom than you did. Didn't you ever see that?"

He looked puzzled for a minute, then he glanced away nervously. "No, I didn't. The two of you were so close, and when she left, I naturally assumed —"

"You assumed! You didn't ask me!"

"But why should I? There was a pattern. I assumed you'd miss her terribly, that I could never take her place in your life. When I was first married to Rachel, I tried everything to get her to be serious, to grow up just a little. Then you came along, and suddenly she had an ally; I couldn't compete. I wanted to take hold of the reins, but by then it was too late. Every time I attempted to get closer to you, she saw it as a restriction I imposed on her. And so I lost out with both of you. I just stopped trying."

"How could you do that?" Becca asked in horror. "How dare you give up on me! You never wanted to hear the truth, Daddy. That's the whole reason for this terrible mess. You can't loosen the reins on me, just the way you couldn't on Mom when she was around, isn't that really it? But I'm not like her, either. I'm Becca! I'm Becca!" She couldn't control her voice anymore. She was sobbing.

Her father shook his head, and she saw him through her tears like a figure vaguely remembered from a dream. "Just because Mom ran away from home," she cried in a flash of understanding, "doesn't mean I'm going to. Don't you know me that well by now? Don't you know anything about me?"

Through her tears, she saw her father's sad, lined face. Was she imagining it, or was he crying, too?

"I know, I know that," he insisted in a choked voice.

"If you can't trust me for a few days away, then we don't have any kind of trust between us at all," she said, wishing she could stop the feelings that were rushing out of her faster than shooting stars. "You just don't ever want me to leave home — isn't that it? Say it, come on, *say it!*" she yelled at the top of her lungs.

"What can I do?" He was still crying and he made no attempt to wipe away the tears that inscribed two deep furrows down his face. "I'm not perfect, Becca. I'm lonely, and I can't bear to think of you leaving, too. Becca, you may not think so, but I love you."

Blindly, her rage and pain mingling with tremendous passion for this man, she gasped and her body went slack. Slowly she came to him and tentatively put her arms around him. How was it possible to feel so many things at one time? She was still terribly angry at him, yet there was something deeper she was just beginning to touch.

"I love you, too, Daddy," she whispered.

His arms went around her, and they held each other fiercely, not daring to let go. After a very long time, he smoothed back a few loose strands of her hair. "Let's not be strangers any-more."

"Never again," she vowed. "I'm so sorry I hurt you."

"We hurt each other," he corrected her. Then he brushed the tears from her cheeks. His touch was kind and loving. But as nice as it was, she couldn't leave it like this. She needed an answer.

"I'm not a baby anymore," she told him gently. "And I don't want you to treat me like one. It doesn't work, you see? Please, will you let me go on the trip?" She pulled the per-mission slip from her pocket and slid it in front of him on the table. He looked at the piece of paper as though it held the secret of life.

He sighed. "I love you enough to let you grow up. I suppose that's the only thing to do."

And then he signed the slip with a flourish.

It was a mild Sunday morning in the first week of March. Becca couldn't help thinking about her mother as she packed carefully, selecting her least crushable and most versa-tile clothes. Rachel had understood — sort of — and had sworn she would make a trip to New York in May.

Becca snapped her suitcase shut at exactly twelve-thirty and carried it out into the hall.

"All ready?" her father asked.

"Uh-huh."

They put on their coats and, without speaking, went downstairs. The car was parked just a few spaces away, up the block. They rode along the empty streets quietly, both of them immersed in their own thoughts. Becca was naturally excited about the trip, but she couldn't help wondering what her father was going to do while she was away.

They had a light lunch at a French bistro on Fiftieth Street called Chez Napoleon, but neither of them finished what was on the plate. The waitress clucked over them and offered to bring them something else, but Dr. Walters assured her that it wasn't the food — the meal was fine. And then he glanced at his daughter and they shared a silent secret.

They drove to Penn Station and parked in a garage across the street.

"Where did your teacher say they were meeting?" the doctor asked as they climbed to the main floor.

"Near Gate 15 up in the waiting area. Oh, there they are!" Becca took his arm and started pulling him along.

"I'd like to speak to Mr. Rydell for a moment, just to make sure I have all the information about where you're staying and on what train you'll be arriving next Saturday."

"Yes, Daddy." Becca didn't say a word about the mimeographed sheets all the students had been given with every conceivable detail. She knew it would make him feel better to check for himself. That was simply the way he was.

Mark was standing on the other side of the waiting room, and he rushed over to take her bag. "Hi, Becca," he grinned. "Hello, Dr. Walters."

"How are you, Mark?" the doctor asked, a little too cheerily, Becca thought. "Ready for the journey?"

"Yeah, I'm pretty excited."

"You'll look after my daughter, I hope," he smiled.

"I'd be delighted, sir."

Becca listened to this interchange, totally amazed. Obviously, her father still thought *someone* had to look after her. But they could talk about that later on.

"I'll be right over there, Becca. I take it that gentleman is your Mr. Rydell?"

"Uh-huh. We'll wait here for you, Daddy."

She shook her head as he walked away briskly.

"What got into him?" Mark asked. "So friendly all of a sudden."

"Something good happened," Becca smiled. "Too hard to explain, but I think things will be better between us from now on. He's not the person he seems to be — he's much more complicated." She sighed. "I didn't really make any attempt to get to know my father, until recently, that is. I guess I had us all mixed up together in my mind. I didn't know if I was making *my* choices or his choices *for* me. But we talked the other night and sort of separated ourselves out. It feels good."

"I bet." Mark clearly didn't understand, but he wasn't going to pry. And Becca, for the first time in a long time, didn't have to spill all the beans. She could keep part of it to herself, to mull over, to grow on, like the extra candle on a birthday cake.

"Well, everything seems in order." Her father approached them tentatively, not wanting to interrupt, but Mark immediately took his cue to get out of the way.

"I'll just get some tags for our suitcases, okay, Becca? I'll see you over by the gate. Remember, it leaves at three on the nose. 'Bye, Dr. Walters."

"In a minute." Becca nodded to Mark as her father murmured his good-bye. Then she turned to him and took his hand.

"So, have a good week," she told him.

"You'll call me every evening before you have dinner and let me know how things are going?"

"Daddy" — she frowned — "I thought you weren't going to sit home every night."

"Well," he admitted, "Ginger did say there was a friend of hers she'd like me to meet. We're all going to the theater together next Tuesday."

"Wonderful!" Becca enthused, feeling only a small pang of strangeness about her father's date.

"I suppose I might even take myself out to dinner alone one night, as a treat," he said.

"I think you should. Okay then, I'll call you tomorrow and Wednesday and Friday. That should be enough, don't you think?" It wasn't really a question, because it was very firmly stated, but even so, Becca was asking his permission.

"Yes, I imagine that would do it."

"I better go now, Daddy. They're starting down the stairs."

"You've got everything? You packed some aspirin and vitamin C, just in case?"

"Everything!" she laughed. "Don't worry, will you?" She put her arms around his neck and drew him close for a kiss. But she didn't break away. Instead, she touched her cheek to his and whispered, "I'll miss you."

"I'll miss you, too, dear. But I know you're going to have a wonderful time on this trip. It's a golden opportunity — something you'll remember for the rest of your life."

She nodded, never thinking to mention that

those had been her very words. The important thing was that he really seemed to be okay about her going.

"Take care. Now don't be late," he called as she hurried off to the gate.

Clutching her purse to her side, she dashed toward the platform. She didn't look back, but she knew that if she had, he would have been there watching, a look of pride and caring suffusing his quiet face.

Her father. Not an ogre, not a hero, just a vulnerable man with the same sorts of problems and emotions that Becca herself had. He was very dear to her, and never more than at that moment when he allowed her to walk away on her own without standing on her shadow. No matter how far they drifted apart after this, they would still be bound tightly together. But the bond was a flexible one, made of mutual understanding and trust and a love that went deeper than their differences. The best part of it was that they could let each other be, to live their own lives without restriction.

I'm not Daddy's little girl. I'm Becca, she thought suddenly, and the idea, although startling, was pretty darn good.

Then Becca reached the platform and she hurried to take her place among her friends. *I wonder what Washington will be like*, she thought, walking with Mark to a seat in the train. *I wonder who we'll meet and what we'll do.*

"Lost in thought again?" Mark demanded as the train started to pull out.

"Thinking," she smiled. "But not lost."

The rumble of the train's wheels grew louder, and they picked up speed, traveling into the soft spring day. For Becca, it was a journey into her future, and whatever happened, she wasn't afraid. She wasn't alone anymore. She had her father. She had Mark. And she would have her mother again, someday.

But most important, she had herself.